the
Big Drift

Center Point
Large Print

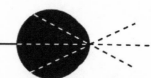

**This Large Print Book carries the
Seal of Approval of N.A.V.H.**

the Big Drift

Patrick Dearen

CENTER POINT LARGE PRINT
THORNDIKE, MAINE

This Center Point Large Print edition is published
in the year 2015 by arrangement with
Texas Christian University Press.

The text of this Large Print edition is unabridged.
In other aspects, this book may vary
from the original edition.
Printed in the United States of America
on permanent paper.
Set in 16-point Times New Roman type.

ISBN: 978-1-62899-560-2

Library of Congress Cataloging-in-Publication Data

Dearen, Patrick.
The big drift / Patrick Dearen. — Center Point Large Print edition.
pages cm
ISBN 978-1-62899-560-2 (library binding : alk. paper)
1. Large type books. I. Title.
PS3554.E1752B54 2015
813′.54—dc23
                                                    2015007643

For John Hyde (1942-2012),
the fairest of judges, the best of men

Our friendship was all too brief,
but I cherished every moment.

Author's Note

In writing about racial aspects of the 1880s, I have tried to balance historical accuracy with modern sensitivities. In so doing, I have consulted the following interviews conducted between 1936 and 1940 with onetime slaves, or first-generation free men, who became cowboys:

Interview Transcripts, Library of Congress,
Manuscript Division,
WPA Federal Writers' Project Collection:
James Cape
Will Crittendon
Tom Garrett
Bones Hooks
Ben Kinchlow
Tom Mills
Sam James Washington

The Cape and Washington interviews, recorded in dialect by Sheldon F. Gauthier in Fort Worth, Texas, provided particularly helpful insights as I developed speech patterns for my character Zeke Boles.

In regard to the Big Drift of 1884 and the ensuing roundup of 1885, I drew largely from primary sources, documented in my nonfiction books *Devils River: Treacherous Twin to the Pecos, 1535-1900* (Fort Worth: TCU Press, 2011), 130-133, and *A Cowboy of the Pecos* (Plano, Texas: Republic of Texas Press, 1997), 171-179.

Master Young! Master Young!

Even across time and distance and over the howl of a bitterly cold norther, Zeke Boles could still hear his own cry as Samuel Young had slumped, bloodying the boardwalk outside the "whites only" tavern. He could still taste the hanging gun smoke and feel the trigger firm against his finger, still see the powder residue that had sprinkled his ebony knuckles. A drunken man's hand also had gripped that Schofield revolver, but only Zeke's had squeezed off the shot that had killed the person who had been the one constant in his twenty-nine years.

And through all the troubling months that had followed Zeke down into West Texas, his only choice had been to run.

The rattle of his spurs in a chilling gust stirred him to the here and now. It was late on a somber day in December 1884, and he hunched half-frozen in the saddle, the nose of his cow pony nodding along through a flurry of snow pellets. Barbed wire flanked his course on the left, and over the bay's ears he could see the posts marching west through broken country marked by prickly pear and the skeletons of dormant scrub mesquites.

It was a drift fence, and bunched against it in places were mossy-horned cattle burned with a Slash Five brand. Denied instinctive retreat from the wintry blast, the beeves could only turn wild eyes and flaring nostrils to the ice-glazed wire and bawl.

The storm's initial dust swirls had caught Zeke by surprise just after he had forded the Middle Concho. When he had swung around in the saddle, the north sky's deep, ominous blue, like bruising on a dead man's face, had told him to brace for the worst. The wind had pushed at his back throughout the two-mile ascent out of the valley, and then the fence had loomed up and turned him west.

Through a freezing mist that had become ice pellets, he had pushed on, searching for sagging wires that he could responsibly stamp down with his boot and step his horse across. Still, Zeke figured that no matter how far he rode from that cattle trail tavern on the Texas side of the distant Big Red, the guilt would go with him. His remorse manifested itself greatest in the money belt, heavy with gold pieces under his moth-eaten coat and linsey-woolsey shirt with missing buttons. With his every heartbeat the belt seemed to throb, most notably where the Schofield revolver in the waistband of his duck pants pushed against it.

It was cursed, this gold of Master Young's, as cursed as the drunken cowhand's revolver that had sent Young to his grave. Only after a half week of day-and-night flight had Zeke even remembered the money, but through all the ensuing miles he had held on to it, not a cent spent, in the vague hope he might somehow return it to the kindly woman who had been the wife of his employer and onetime master.

Zeke tilted his sweat-stained hat against the wind and drew his coat tighter across his shoulders. Still, he shuddered, for more reasons than one. For days he had weighed responsibility against haunting reminder, but ever since the Middle Concho, the piercing cold had seemed bent on crushing what little remained of his tenuous sense of duty. The money belt and revolver were killing him, one punishing memory at a time, and he would never rest again until he rid himself of both.

About that time Zeke rode upon a cattle carcass beside the barbed strands where the beef had weakened and died a winter or two before. The buzzards and maggots had done their job, and now only shreds of jerky and parchment-like skin clung to the partially exposed rib cage.

Zeke pulled rein and dismounted stiffly. He

11

had little circulation, his legs as numb as his wind-chapped face, and he paused to rub the back of his thigh before snubbing his horse to a post.

Turning to the carcass, he withdrew the forty-five. Funny how the feel of the grip's curvature made that awful scene outside the tavern so much more vivid—the confusion and shock in Master Young's gray eyes, his bright blood smearing the pillar as he had slid down it, the quick spasm and then utter stillness as he had lain on that boardwalk oozing red.

The blue Schofield with the seven-inch barrel began to tremble in Zeke's hand. The ground tugged at the weapon and he let it fall, an instrument of death that abruptly stared up from his feet like a window into hell. Opening his coat and shirt to the ripping wind, he unbuckled the money belt. The leather was stubborn, caught in his waistband, and he yanked frantically, finally shedding the belt as if it were a snake. The falling snow began to dust it on the ground, but Zeke made himself retrieve it, a dangling three footer still rattling as the coins shifted.

Kneeling to the frozen carcass, Zeke fed the belt through a break in the rib cage. The Schofield, he scooped up and inserted next, and then he stuffed the cursed items as deep in the concealing bowels as possible.

He already felt better as he untied his horse and slipped his boot in the stirrup. But even as he threw a leg over the saddle, he heard something down the fence line that gave him pause. Here on the rim of the Middle Concho basin, the barbed wire alternately dropped into catclaw-infested drainages and climbed elevated shoulders of rock and cacti. Just such a rise lay ahead, hiding the distance, but it couldn't muffle the scream of a horse in distress.

Zeke had been a cowhand since age fourteen, when he had first helped point Master Young's cattle up from South Texas to Kansas. Even then, the older cowhands had marveled at his horsemanship. In appreciation of his way with a greenbroke horse, Master Young had dubbed him a "riding fool." Part of the reason had been Zeke's natural athleticism, but he also had an innate affinity for horses and could, as Master Young used to say, coax more out of a clabber-head bronc than any other rider he had ever seen.

So it was not surprising now that Zeke urged the bay up the rocky slope to do what he could for the crying animal. He heard wire snap and a frantic stirring that raised sweeping dust, and then he topped out in tasajillo and prickly pear to see driving snow pellets shrouding a fence line rider's worst nightmare. Not far below, a horseman was down, and so was his roan, the two of them hopelessly caught up in barbed wire. Streaming red, the horse was on its side, and the white cowhand pinned underneath was desperately trying to still the flailing animal as the barbs raked and bloodied.

"Hyaah!"

Zeke touched spurs to horsehide, and rider and animal barreled down the slope. He hadn't seen anything so troubling since the forty-five's muzzle had exploded during the struggle with the drunken cowhand. Ten yards shy of the wreck, he reined up so forcefully that his bay almost sat on its haunches, and then he was off the bronc and securing the reins to the fence.

"I help you!" Zeke's only education had come in Master Young's East Texas cotton fields, and even after fifteen years of cowboying, his dialect still told of those early days as a slave.

Time was critical, but he forced himself to approach slowly, not wanting to terrify the downed horse more. As it was, the snorting pony thrashed wildly, punishing the ashen cowhand who fought futilely to bring its head around to its shoulder, the only position in which he might control the animal. But the wide-eyed rider just didn't have the leverage, not with his arms and the roan's neck twisted in barbed wire. With every toss of the horse's lacerated head, every whip of its strong legs, the barbs shredded the cowhand's coat more.

Zeke knew that this was one horse he wouldn't be able to talk down. He extended a helpless arm, and then through the melee he caught the trapped rider's eyes.

"Do what you got to!" cried the man.

Zeke knew what that had to be, for a rifle butt showed in a scabbard under the pitching saddle. Lunging, he took a beating from powerful bone and sinew, but when he fell away he had a Winchester carbine in his hand.

Even as he scrambled up, he worked the lever and threw a cartridge in the chamber. Timing the violent heave of the roan's head, he drove the barrel between the snake-blood eyes and squeezed the trigger.

The blast rattled Zeke's eardrums, the recoil driving into his shoulder. His own startled horse almost broke free, but the animal before the muzzle grew still.

Zeke faced a cowhand in his late twenties whose chest labored like bellows. "You all right?"

Blue eyes that suddenly seemed as haunted as Zeke's locked on him.

"You' leg," continued Zeke, leaning the rifle against a post. "You broke up?"

Whatever spell that had seized the cowhand relaxed a little. "Swell of the saddle saved me."

With a cut hand, the man with the blood-splattered stubble and sandy hair tried futilely to ease the tension of a wicked barbed loop around his arm. He glanced up furtively. "Some snips in my war bag."

Zeke sought out a leather pouch on the felled

animal's saddle and located wire cutters. Stepping across the carcass with its blood-flecked foam, he started to sever the wire at the cowhand's shoulder, but with an impatient "Uh-uh," the man waved him off.

Zeke relinquished the snips and backed away, giving the man space. As the cowhand awkwardly began cutting himself free, Zeke turned to his bay and took up his catch-rope. Working the noose over the dead roan's head, he snugged it against the sweaty neck and then untied his horse and mounted up.

Zeke took up the slack with a few turns around the saddle horn and sat shivering as he watched the cowhand painstakingly cut away. Finally, the last length of wire popped and the man was loose. The cowhand looked up, the only signal Zeke needed to back his horse, the rope slipping a little around the horn as it tightened. Within seconds, he had dragged the carcass far enough for the man to wrench his leg free.

Zeke started to dismount and seek his rope, but the cowhand discouraged him with an outstretched palm as though again reluctant to accept more help than he had to. After gaining his feet and testing his leg, the man loosed the lariat and allowed Zeke to reel it in.

"You got a place to go?" Zeke asked as he tied the coil to his saddle.

The haunted blue eyes looked up at him.

"We got a bad one on us," Zeke continued, glancing back at the north sky. "Like as not freeze to death afoot."

The cowhand stared. Zeke scooted forward against the horn and patted the seat behind him.

"Here you go," he said. "Hitch you'self a ride."

The man glanced at the dead horse and then surveyed the frozen countryside. Zeke could see a lot of contemplation in his still-ashen features. Finally, the cowhand found his worn hat and Winchester and approached as if it were the last thing he wanted to do.

Zeke removed his left boot from the stirrup and allowed the man to step on.

"Slash Fives is thataway," muttered the cowhand.

Zeke glanced over his shoulder and saw a bleeding finger pointing to the Middle Concho lowlands. "You with the Slash Fives?"

The only reply was the howl of the wind, and with a creak of leather, Zeke turned a little more in the saddle so that they faced one another.

"They call me Zeke."

Once more, the man fixed his troubled gaze on Zeke, but his focus seemed on something far away.

"Line shack across the Concho yonder," he finally allowed.

"Yes, sir," said Zeke, reining his horse into the teeth of a growing blizzard. "We sure better ride."

2

Unclean.

There was no other way to describe how Will Brite felt as he bounced in the saddle behind the angular black stranger with high-cut cheekbones and long, wiry legs that demanded his stirrups ride low. Will steadied himself with a hand to the cantle at his back, but even as he tried to keep his balance, he resisted the temptation to grip the Negro's coat.

The descent toward the Concho was rugged, and through his thighs Will could feel the bay struggle. The double weight was a load on the ridden-down animal, but the burden on Will's conscience was a hell of a lot worse.

He shivered, and it wasn't just because he faced a relentless wind that seemed intent on chilling him to the bone. He remembered a night on a Texarkana farm nineteen years before, and a bucket of kerosene that he had doused on the sagging porch of a wood-frame shack set against dogwood shrubs crawling with rattan. He had been only a boy of ten, but he had done a grown man's evil, and he could still smell the kerosene and see the puddle spread across the rotting planks.

Pa! Pa! Why we doin' this, Pa?

But his father wouldn't answer his frantic whisper, even as the man splashed the rickety door and shuttered window with kerosene from a second bucket. Then a match flared against those only means of exit, and young Will fell back with his pa to watch hell on earth.

The flames against night . . . the roar as they devoured groaning wood . . . the thick, acrid smoke that choked Will's throat . . . the rumble under his feet as timbers collapsed. . . . As indelibly burned on his memory as all these details were, they were nothing compared to the awful screams that still raged in Will's ears.

Will was unclean, all right, so much so that he knew there must be a special place in hell for him. And he had only the Negro who called himself Zeke to blame for this terrible reminder of pending judgment.

Nevertheless, he owed this black man his life, and Will's emotions were a whirling mill of resentment and gratitude, anger and guilt.

With infrequent arm signals and even rarer words, Will guided Zeke down into the lowlands. The wind persisted, no less vicious behind the stranger's shielding shoulders. Will hadn't experienced a winter on the Middle Concho before; he had drifted in from the South Texas

Brush Country and signed on with the Slash Fives only last spring. Still, from what other Slash Five riders had told him of winters here, he figured this storm had the makings of the kind of blizzard this country hadn't seen in a long time.

If so, he hoped the drift fence would do its job for the Slash Fives and the outfits north of it. This was still open range, save for the thirty miles of barbed wire that was all that stood between the Middle Concho and a no-man's-land to the south. Nearly a hundred miles of it and dry all the way, so Will had heard, and at the end waited a river so treacherous that only one name would fit—the Devils.

But maybe the devil had already claimed a lot more than some far-off stream.

Ever since Will and Wampus had holed up for winter in the line shack, the two of them had ridden the fence and made repairs. The fence was really owned by the cattleman's association, but because it constituted the ranch's south boundary, the Slash Fives had a vested interest in keeping it up. Sometimes Will and Wampus rode together, especially if they had already identified a stretch that needed mending, but on this day Wampus had headed west and Will had gone east.

A tangle of old wire on the ground and a bronc notorious for "seeing snakes"—it had been the perfect recipe for disaster. When the spooked roan had tripped and Will had gone down against the fence, he had wondered if somebody up above had figured up his time. With a firearm normally a liability when brush could snag it, the only reason he had even carried the Winchester was because he had seen a loafer wolf the day before. Lucky or not, he knew he damned sure didn't deserve to be saved by a colored man.

By the time Zeke's bay splashed across the shallow Concho just upstream of the tossing limbs of a bare pecan, a virtual whiteout descended. Will had seen a few snows in his time, but never had he experienced anything like this. The bay's ears were only a couple of feet past Zeke's shoulder, yet they seemed to dance in and out of a violent sea of white. The flurries blinded and whipped and suffocated, and all Will could do was yell in Zeke's ear and urge him to hold his course.

A couple of hundred yards past the river, a ghostly shape rose up at ten o'clock, and to Will's nudge and a sweep of his arm, the Negro reined the bay toward it. Will was aware when the horse tried to wheel and go with the wind, just as he also knew when Zeke applied punishing spurs to control the cold-jawing animal.

The camp consisted of a sagging, twelve-by-fourteen cabin, a west-side shed, and an adjoining two-acre trap, but they were almost there before Will could make out anything other than the mere suggestion of a structure. The box-and-strip shack with shuttered windows faced north, and when they negotiated the corner and reached the stacked rocks at the door, Will discerned the fleeting outline of a man unsaddling a horse at the shed twenty yards away.

Will swung down off the bay and started to mount the ice-glazed rocks that served as steps. It would have been so easy to push open the door and forget about this black stranger, so easy to run from the memories and pretend that none of it had ever happened.

But he couldn't.

He pointed to the shed. "Over yonder by Wampus," he shouted. "Unsaddle him, turn him in the trap."

"I holes up in the shed if it's all right," said Zeke.

"Yeah."

Will turned to the door, the guilt building. Whirling, he caught the black man's arm just as he started to ride away.

"You come . . ." Will hesitated, and then forced out the words. "You get done, come on in."

Not waiting for a response, he reached for the door knob. He had made the offer, and that was all it took to assuage his conscience. Still, Will hoped he never saw him again.

Blowing snow followed him into a murky room that grew darker as he closed the door. He felt his way across to a rickety table, removed the globe of a coal-oil lamp, and struck a match from his shirt pocket. As he lighted the wick and slipped the globe back into place, the flame illuminated a rustic room with a couple of cots and a cast iron stove with a flue pipe that extended through an open-rafter ceiling. The shack was like an icebox, and even behind a closed door and shuttered windows, enough wind whistled through to make the lamp flicker.

Gathering mesquite wood from the corner, Will stoked the stove and lighted it with kindling. As he adjusted the damper, a blast of arctic air burst in from behind and extinguished the lamp. Turning, Will saw Wampus stamping snow from his boots in the open doorway.

"What's goin' on? Come in double? Who the hell's the colored boy?"

The gruff words came rapid-fire, as the cowhand always talked, and the bunched questions without waiting for answers was also just like Wampus, who seemed to enjoy hearing himself chatter. A stocky thirty-year-old with a perpetually flushed face, bulging veins, and wild, bloodshot eyes, Wampus always looked the part of someone itching for a fight. Will knew that his line-shack partner was mostly bluster, and sometimes he even delighted in egging the hothead on. But Will was in no mood today for even a semblance of patience.

"Want to shut the damned door?" Will snapped.

Even as he complied, Wampus fired more questions. "How come you in the dark? Light the lamp, why don't you? Got cat eyes or somethin'?"

Will just breathed sharply and re-lighted the lamp; some things weren't worth augering about with a yahoo.

"Said, who's the colored boy?" Wampus asked again as he untied his chaps. "Where's the roan you rode out on?"

Will started for his cot against the west wall, but stopped to linger by the building heat of the crackling stove.

"Pulled me out of a jam," he said quietly.

He started to remove his leggings, and then hesitated, to reflect. The truth was, he would be headed to a shallow grave right now if not for Zeke.

"Got my horse killed," he added. "Have to go back out for my saddle when the weather breaks."

"Must've been a helluva stunt you pulled. Slash Fives ain't hired him on, has they? Used to work with a darkie on the Brazos. Laziest SOB ever was."

"Wouldn't want to judge ever' man by one," countered Will, casting an accusing glance that went unnoticed. "He seems to—"

Will caught himself. Why was he defending a colored man that way? For the last nineteen years Will had avoided Negroes like cholera.

"Got them damned Yankees to blame for turnin' 'em loose on us in the first place," said Wampus. "Worse than chuck-line riders—never could fend for theirselves."

Will removed his leggings and hung them from a nail at the head of his cot. He wished Wampus would shut up; his words were too similar to what his father had said all those guilt-ridden years ago.

"Here we are in here," Wampus railed on, "while he's out there probably stealin' us blind. You tell him he could stay in the tack house?"

Will plopped down on the squeaking cot, his head sagging as he rested forearms across knees.

"Told him more than that," he muttered wearily, more beaten down by the topic of conversation than by the ordeal he had just undergone.

"Huh?"

A knock sounded at the door, piercing Will as if it had been a cattle prod, but it was Wampus who reacted vocally.

"What the hell—"

His spurs jingling, Wampus went to the door and opened it a mere crack, the wind squealing through as he peeked out. Will couldn't see outside, but there was something in Wampus's body language that reminded him of a horned toad swelling up before it spits blood from its eye.

For the longest Wampus just stared before Will heard a meek voice through the door.

"I was told come back."

"What the hell for?" Wampus snapped. "This ain't no chuck line. Vamoose."

Wampus shut the door and went to his cot. Will, his conscience pricked again, alternately looked at the door and the cowhand, who propped first one boot on the cot frame and then the other as he unbuckled his spurs. Turning to the stove, Will studied the glowing cracks in the cast iron and felt the radiating heat that seemed so powerless against a strange inner chill.

"Not right to turn a man out in this," he said quietly.

Wampus glanced over his shoulder, his only response before tossing his spurs down behind a cot leg.

"Need to . . . Need to let him in," Will went on, as much to convince himself as Wampus.

Wampus snorted as he straightened his rumpled blankets. "Ain't like he's a white man or somethin'. I've spent a-many a night out in the cold."

The entire house seemed to shake in a fierce gust, and Will fixed his gaze on the door again. If the Negro had just never come back to the steps . . . if he had just never offered Will a ride . . . hell, if he had just never happened on Will's horse wreck in the first place. . . .

Yeah if never, thought Will, knowing full well the consequences.

He stood and went to the door. The knob was

like ice as he opened to a blizzard even worse than before, the snow swirling and choking. The wind burned as he pulled his hat down over his face and started into it. With day dying, there wasn't even the suggestion of a shed anymore, but he knew where it lay. The thing was, if a man miscalculated in a storm like this, he could wander off and lose a lot more than his way.

His boots padded through a thickening white cushion as he counted his steps. He must have figured right, for the open-sided shed suddenly rose up, just a hint of a shadow that was there one moment and gone the next.

"You in there?" he shouted, the words drowned out by the wind.

The eave was too low for a man of normal height, but after Will ducked and advanced a couple of steps, he could stand erect again. Still, the rhythmic bang of loose tin right above his head was almost loud enough to keep a person from hearing his own thoughts.

A part of Will didn't want to call out for the stranger by name, for to do so would be to admit that Zeke was a fellow struggler with the same kind of hopes and dreams. If he could just keep from humanizing this Negro, continue to cling to the notion that his race was something less, then maybe it would lessen the terrible regret.

"Zeke?" Will asked, surprising himself. "You in here?"

Will saw movement before he heard a reply that he couldn't distinguish. He went closer, brushing bridles hanging from a rafter, and saw a form rising against saddles piled against the far wall. Zeke had wrapped himself in an old horse blanket, but his shoulders still shook as he faced Will.

"You come on in with me," said Will.

"Boss man done say git."

"Wampus isn't boss. Just tries to act like it sometimes."

"I better stays put. I be gone when the cock-a-doodle hollers."

Again, Will had a reason to turn away and forget, or at least try. But even behind this clattering windbreak, the cold was frightful enough to peel a man's flesh from his face. He bet that dead horse of his was already frozen solid.

Will took his arm. "Come on."

They started for the house, the wind knifing through Will's duck trousers the moment the two of them stepped out of the shed. Will's hands ached so much that he couldn't wait to get in front of the stove again, but all he could do for now was shove them inside his coat pockets and tough it out. He tolled off his steps again—five, eight, a dozen—as the descending dusk robbed more and more of the already limited visibility. He was almost certain they had missed the shack until he kicked the stacked rocks, and then he felt for the door knob and found it.

"Here!" he shouted.

Will would never have believed that he could care a lick about what Wampus thought, but he dreaded like hell going in. An unwritten rule around the chuck wagon was that Mexicans—no matter how respected they might be for their cowboying abilities—were always to segregate themselves on the wagon tongue at grub time, rather than eat with the white cowhands. When it came to sharing a line shack in winter, the boss always paired Mexican with Mexican and white with white. The practice was so accepted that everyone just took it for granted. And while Will had never cowboyed with a Negro, he couldn't imagine the custom being any different. If anything, the lines would have been ever more sharply drawn, for Negroes were less than twenty years removed from slavery and no one had forgotten.

His gaze dropping, Will pushed open the door and went in stamping his feet. He knew when Zeke crossed the threshold after him, for the snow began to fly from a second pair of pounding boots. Closing the door and looking up, Will found Wampus standing there with that same horned toad swell in his face.

"What the hell's this?" Wampus demanded.

Will headed straight for the stove, the click of

29

the black man's boot heels echoing his every step.

"I don't want him in here, Will," Wampus went on.

Will checked the fire, and then sought out the wood pile in the corner. Selecting a gnarled log, he handed it to Zeke, who lingered beside the stove.

"Said, I don't want him in here," Wampus repeated.

"Nobody asked you what you wanted," said Will, watching the stranger kneel to stoke the fire. "Name's Zeke. Won't have to worry about him in the tack house now."

"Least out there he couldn't get to our pokes. That one on the Brazos got away with damned near ever' cent I had."

"He's stayin'."

"Yeah? Who made you boss of this outfit? Probably covered in lice."

"I just goes back to the shed," spoke up Zeke, looking up from the stove.

Will had now invited, insisted on, and defended the stranger's presence, when so many things inside of him screamed that he not. Surely he had done all that his conscience demanded, that his soul demanded, but then he saw the firelight playing in a face as black as that Texarkana night.

"Some people's all bark," Will told Zeke. "Pick you a spot out and I'll grab you a blanket and some beans."

"The hell I don't bite," grumbled Wampus. "I know one thing—he better put a 'Mister' in front of our names."

From well-stocked shelves against the back wall, Will pulled out three tins, but no sooner had he split the tops with his pocketknife than he heard a low drone that reminded him of a far-off freight train. It was a three-day ride to the nearest railroad, but a fellow could hear almost anything in a wind. Baching in a remote Brush Country camp one winter, Will had alternately heard a choir, the murmur of a crowd, and a girl's sweet whisper in the night gusts.

He went ahead and emptied the cans into a rusty iron skillet, but hesitated as he turned with it to the stove. Not only was the rumble growing more distinct, there seemed to be two tones to it—an underlying drumming, and a lilting, deep-throated call. He could almost feel it right through the floor, and he lifted his gaze in wonderment to the door.

"Hants, Mister Will. They . . . They's hants out there."

There was a tremble in Zeke's voice, and when Will looked at the Negro, he saw the lamp's glow illuminating a pair of wide eyes starkly white against his ebony face.

Plopping the skillet down on the stove, Will hurried to the door and threw it open to a dusk suddenly filled with more than a fierce and chilling blizzard. Thundering and bawling, a great shadow that seemed composed of many smaller shadows rushed pell-mell toward him, splitting almost in his very face to surge left and right by the line shack.

"Hants, hell!" Wampus exclaimed from his shoulder. "Storm's got ever' cow in the country runnin' from it!"

3

Curled in a ragged blanket on the floor near the stove, Zeke shivered and slept and shivered. A chill seeped through the underlying cracks and penetrated his marrow, but at least this was the kind of cold that a man could endure, although his numb feet might have argued differently.

Dusk's engine of destruction had lasted only a couple of minutes, but even after Will had blown out the lamp and the two Slash Five hands had lapsed into sleep, Zeke had lain awake, smelling the mesquite smoke and contemplating. He already had come to grips with the fact that the rushing wave had constituted cattle, not spirits, for he had experienced too many stampedes on the trail to Kansas over the years. But what kept him tossing on the hard floor was the realization that once more he had let himself get caught up in a confrontation between two white men. The last time, Master Young had died, and Zeke didn't want any more blood on his conscience.

The running cattle had forestalled any real trouble between the Slash Five hands, but Zeke knew that things could change in a hurry if he stayed around long. Only after he made up his mind to leave at first light, no matter the weather, did he finally get substantive sleep. Still, an image of Master Young bleeding out on those planks kept flashing in his dreams.

Will awoke to a banging at the door and a realization of how cold he was without the blanket he had loaned Zeke. With the windows shuttered, he couldn't tell if day had broken, but his inner sense of time told him that it had. He had slept fully clothed, knowing the fire would burn down, so all he had to do was slip on his boots. What he hadn't expected was all the soreness from the horse wreck, but it was there in heaps as he tugged at the leather uppers.

Will hadn't known that boots could freeze, but they were like blocks of ice as he made his way across the creaking floor. He opened it to a ferocious wind blowing snow out of a white dawn that served as backdrop for a pair of familiar faces.

"Hope you got a fire going, Will," said the nearer, a fifty-ish man with craggy features of experience and intelligent gray eyes. He was Major Hyler, who managed the Slash Fives for a New York syndicate. Will didn't know if "Major" was his given name, a onetime military rank, or just one of those honorary titles that a man sometimes earned through accomplishment and respect. Something in Hyler's square jaw and bearing made Will want to respect him, all right, even if the older man was more cowman than cowboy. Cow work could be learned, but Hyler had a business savvy that was beyond a simple cowhand.

"Out of the snows two men rode," quoted a short, wiry man of mid-thirties who stood behind the Major. "A harder day, winter never sowed."

Even if Will hadn't seen Arch Brannon, he would have recognized him by his unusual speech pattern. Arch had made his living skinning buffalo before the great herds had disappeared in the late seventies, and for all that Arch had to say about his doings before that time, he might as well have sprung into life as a grown man with a skinning knife in hand. Still, Will had always figured him for a onetime schoolteacher, even if that made Arch a study in contradictions, considering the hide industry's reputation for illiterate, hard-swearing men. Nevertheless, all those days of wallowing in buffalo carcasses had left Arch with a body odor that not even lye soap could wash away.

Even as Will stepped aside to let the men in, he was embarrassed, even ashamed, that they too would learn about Zeke. He didn't know what to say, so he retreated to the table and removed the smutty globe from the lamp. As he heard the door close and the two visitors exchange greetings with a stirring Wampus, he lighted the wick so that shadows began to flicker against the walls.

"Worried about those cows," said Hyler. "We started out from headquarters soon as we thought our horses could find their way."

"Never saw nothin' like it," Wampus said. "Dusk settle in, here they come stompedin' right through our camp."

"The hell they did!" said Hyler. "If that drift fence doesn't hold. . . ."

"What manner guest stirs there, Will?"

At Arch's voice, Will looked at Zeke, who had sat up on the floor. "See if you can get a fire goin'," Will told him.

Zeke took a moment to reach for his boots, giving Will an excuse to start for the corner wood pile.

"That Will always was a fool about chasin' after strays," snapped Wampus.

Will secured a little wood, and as he turned back to the stove, he saw Hyler and the Negro standing face-to-face.

"What they call you, boy?" asked Hyler.

"Zeke."

"I tell you, Zeke, we got our work cut out for us, those cattle scattering like they are," said Hyler. "What kind of hand you make? You looking?"

Will flinched and focused on Zeke. *No! Tell him no!*

Even from his angle, Will could read hesitation

36

in the stranger's face. The ranch manager must have seen it too, for he pressed the matter.

"Answer me, Zeke. You a cowhand?"

"Yes, sir, since I was a young'n."

"Consider it day work if you don't want to stay. Long as you're here, pay's six bits a day and found. Now let's all get some hot coffee down us and take out after those cows."

As the five of them reined their horses south from the trap, Zeke figured the snow for six or seven inches deep, enough to bury a hoof with every step. Even worse, more snow was falling, carried on a barreling wind that cut right through his coat. Pushing at his back, it was at least bearable, but Zeke already dreaded turning around eventually and facing it.

At least visibility was somewhat better today, although the blanket of white on the ground and the coating of ice on every algerita branch and mesquite thorn tricked a man into believing it was even colder than it really was. But Zeke wasn't so sure that was possible, the way his breath clouded and his thighs ached to the feel of the frozen saddle.

By now, Zeke had hoped to be bearing south on his own again, putting more distance between that Red River tavern and him. But something about Major Hyler reminded Zeke of Master Young. Maybe it was the way he set his jaw so firmly when he talked, or the way the scoring in his forehead deepened when he spoke of how the cows had to be suffering in all of this. Over the years, Zeke had come to realize that the best measure of a man's character was how he treated horses and cattle, and Zeke liked what he had seen so far.

They were only halfway to the river when Zeke pulled rein. He seemed to hear the telltale sound before anyone else, for the other riders began pulling away. He scanned the wild plum trees and gooseberry vines lining the bank to the west, the bottomland with all the catclaw interspersed with mesquite, the ridges, bunched by distance, that angled up out of the valley as if supporting the bordering hills to the north. Near the crest he could make out three or four cedars, dark green specks in the snow. None of that could explain the abrupt humming and accompanying chorus, but Zeke now knew that something a lot more tangible than ghosts was involved.

Then it came surging, a swift and ominous shadow pouring off the crest. Stark against the white, it swamped the upper slope like a tidal wave across Master Young's Gulf Coast fields. The shadow's nearer side was maybe a half-mile away, making it difficult for Zeke to get much of a perspective. But he could see that the leading edge was a series of thin fingers, reaching and taking, opening the way for a great, pulsing body of cattle that must have been a mile wide as it raced down ridge and gully.

Zeke couldn't find words, but his companions found enough for all of them.

"Over yonder!"

"What in hell!"

"Lord Almighty!"

"Let's work our way over there!"

The last cry came from Hyler, but Zeke didn't need any urging. Already, he had his Slash Five Appaloosa cutting trail through the snow.

"Crazy as devils cast in a herd of swine!" observed Arch.

"Sure got their tails to the wind, all right!" said Will. "How long can mossy-horns keep up that trot?"

Zeke knew for a fact. "Awful long way, Mister Will. One time I seen 'em run ten mile goin' all-out."

"Hell, you ain't seen nothin' of the kind," snapped Wampus.

Zeke went silent; he had learned the hard way not to cross a white man.

"I expect he knows what he's seen," spoke up Will. "I—"

Will seemed ready to say more, but he didn't. Still, Zeke hadn't figured on anybody defending him, and he glanced back in surprise and found Will looking down.

"One thing's for sure," said Hyler. "They're

sure burning off the flesh. That's pure-dee money they're dropping, boys."

"Only way they's got of stayin' alive, I reckon," said Zeke. "They's gotta run from the storm, and if they's can't run no more, they's freeze to death standin' up."

Wampus snorted. "Just full of big windies, ain't he?"

"I would hesitate judging so quickly, Wampus," interjected Arch. "I've read of soldiers frozen solid, sitting up holding their rifles."

Still, it wasn't enough for Wampus, who reminded Zeke of one particularly ornery mule back in his early years on Master Young's plantation.

"Sittin's one thing," Wampus contended. "What's gonna hold up a froze cow?"

"Perhaps four legs?" suggested Arch.

Soon they were close enough to make out individual beeves and hear the clash of horns amid the collective bawling and the snow-muffled pounding of thousands of hoofs. Zeke had never seen so many cattle. The whole world seemed filled with them already, and yet they continued to rush off the summit. There was nothing in Zeke's experience with which to compare their numbers, except maybe grains of grit in the blackest of sandstorms.

"Any Slash Five brands?" shouted Hyler as the riders closed to within fifty yards.

Zeke knew that a stampede always took on a life of its own, dictated by mysterious whims that somehow possessed every beef at the same instant. He had never witnessed this level of mass migration before, but he figured that the forces that controlled it were just as unpredictable.

He pulled rein, keeping that fifty-yard buffer, and studied the rampaging animals for brands. They were all longhorns, the only breed that could sustain such flight, even if their tongues already hung out as their flaring nostrils slung slimy streamers. No matter that theirs was a trot and not a run, they had the kind of stampede devils in their eyes that told Zeke it was impossible to turn them back. The flinty hoofs just kept churning, bowling over mesquites and uprooting cacti and anything else that stood in their way.

"Lots of brands," said Will, who had pulled up at Zeke's right. "But don't see no Slash—"

"Watch out!"

Zeke's attention was on the passing blur of hides and horns, but at Hyler's cry he looked past Will's hunched form in the saddle and saw disaster coming. Halfway up the adjacent hill, one of those inexplicable whims had seized the outer edge of the herd, and the possessed eyes were storming hell-bent straight toward them.

Zeke knew that if a man afoot could muster the courage to hold his ground, charging cattle ordinarily would sidestep him until the entire herd had passed. But he and the Slash Five hands were on horseback, and the broncs between their legs were already unnerved by the bedlam. Furthermore, a horse was a herd animal with the same instinct for group flight as a bovine, and to expect a bronc to stand calmly in place was too much to ask. If a horse shied just a hair to one side or the other, it could step in the path of a dodging steer with deadly consequences.

With only one choice, Zeke wheeled the Appaloosa and applied spurs.

"We gotta git!"

But the others already were whirling their mounts as catclaw and mesquite slapped his chaps. Retreating at a right angle to the cattle, every cowhand should have escaped, but the thundering beeves had other ideas. Maybe the stampede devils were influenced by the course of the horses; Zeke didn't waste time pondering. He only had to look from summit to lowlands and see the entire raging shadow break sharply toward him to know to brace for the worst.

Now the race was desperate, Zeke's Appaloosa and Will's bay running side by side through a spray of snow kicked up by the lead horses. Suddenly there were as many cattle ahead as at the two men's flank, all of them poised to broadside Will's mount and plow through to Zeke's.

At the last instant, Zeke shouted a warning and turned his Appaloosa to run with the cattle, the only thing he could do to avoid a collision. Still, within moments he and the Appaloosa were caught up in a terrifying mass of flashing horns and jostling brutes that carried them along, helpless victims in a great, surging flood. To go down would be to face an awful death under a crush of sharp hoofs, but all Zeke could do was give the Appaloosa its head and cling to fragile hope.

Maybe it wasn't hope that was fragile, but life. Zeke remembered a dark night on the Arkansas when a milling herd had swallowed a fifteen-year-old rider. The boy's empty horse had worked its way out about midnight, but Zeke and the other cowhands had been forced to wait until the cattle had settled down at daybreak to ride in and search. Trampled all night long, the poor boy's body had been the most horrible thing Zeke had ever seen. He just prayed now that if it came to it, the end would be as quick and merciful as a single hoof to the skull.

Merciful.

Sure, Master Young, I deserve somethin', all right, but mercy it ain't.

But even while Zeke rocked to the bump of so many cattle and winced to the flail of horns gouging out space, he sensed an ironic advantage to this forsaken moment. A frenzied herd gave

off a tremendous amount of heat, enough to offset some of the bone-piercing chill on this coldest
of days.

He glimpsed Will and a couple of other riders,
their mounts tossing in the fringe of a relentless
sea that swept them on and on. Communication
was impossible, but what could any of them have
said except a backsliding cowboy's prayer?

Suddenly the flow of crazed beeves seemed to
strike a ripple ahead. Every backbone and
curving horn dropped, and when the speckled
frames rose again another twenty yards farther,
the herd was a little thinner but no less frantic.
One more stride and Zeke rode only air for a
moment, as though a powerful force had yanked
the horse out from under him even as his boots
stayed in the stirrups. The sensation lasted only
an instant before saddle leather hit his buttocks,
simultaneous with a splash of water and then a
mist more blinding than the swirling snow.

Zeke knew his horse had just plunged down the
riverbank, but he had a lot more to worry about
than the Concho shallows. The waters were
almost dammed by fallen beeves, their sinewy
frames floundering in useless fight against the
onslaught of hoofs. The squealing Appaloosa
twisted and reared, almost throwing Zeke.
Somehow he managed to hold on, but now the
hurrying mass of upright beeves tightened again,
leaving no place for the horse's pawing forelegs

to drop except astride the hindquarters of the stumbling longhorn ahead.

With Zeke clinging to the saddle horn for the wildest moment of his life, his horse half-rode the unwitting steer on across the stream and halfway up the bank before its unshod hoofs slid off to solid footing again.

The Concho was behind Zeke now, but he was still at the mercy of a rushing river. The beeves bore him across the trampled brush of the valley and funneled him up through a rugged drainage into south-lying hills. For harried minutes Zeke held out hope that the sharp ascent would compel the animals to halt, but the constant push of cattle from behind remained an unstoppable force. They slowed a little as they climbed, but it only served to squeeze the beeves closer until Zeke could feel crushing weight against both legs.

He had yet to give any thought to what would happen when the leaders struck the drift fence; just staying alive from one stride to the next had been worry enough. But as the uplift began to level off, he realized the wire had to be getting close. Then the leaders topped out fifty yards ahead only to rise even more sharply, creating a strange wall of cow hides. It was as though something had buckled this hurtling train, leaving no other place for its compact parts to go but skyward.

Zeke intuitively sensed what was happening—the leaders had burst upon those wicked barbs. They had planted their forefeet, and every bovine in their wake had plowed into the animal in front of it. Successive waves of beeves were falling in a swelling heap, forming a stair-stepping course of hide, hair, and horns for the beeves that charged after them.

The herd's momentum carried Zeke's Appaloosa right on up that jumbled mound of carcasses, and the moment the horse plunged off the far side, Zeke had his answer to the drift fence question. By the dead and the dying, he and the surviving cattle had bridged the barrier, and now they had nothing before them but a wilderness of white.

No sooner did the Appaloosa's hoofs pound the packed snow again than Zeke realized an advantage in this half-speed stampede. So many beeves had gone down that he was within twenty-five yards of the new leaders. Not only that, but the onrushing herd had thinned enough to maneuver a little.

Spurring his horse, Zeke began to advance. It was tricky, weaving through all the shifting forms and strafing horns, but suddenly the Appaloosa's nose was in the tail of one of the leaders. Zeke held his horse there, waiting and hoping, and then a split developed on the steer's flank and he went for it. Brushing cow hide and feeling the drag of a horn across his thigh, he broke into the lead and opened up his horse.

Zeke could only hope that the snow didn't hide a badger hole or a prairie dog town. Footing underneath was treacherous enough as it was, and more than once the Appaloosa stumbled and lost stride. With glances back, Zeke gauged his growing separation from the herd and finally cut the bronc to the left, knowing now that he could angle across and escape.

Zeke kept his horse in a gallop for several hundred yards before he felt secure enough to ease the laboring animal into a walk. Turning into the wind, he started toward the fence in search of his companions. He realized that he hadn't seen any of them since the river, and a quick scan of the migrating herd gave him no clues. If they hadn't been as lucky. . . .

Zeke cringed at the thought of working his way back along the stampede path and finding the mangled bodies of fellow cowhands, but he would do what he had to once the herd passed.

He struck an intact stretch of fence and pulled rein. A few hundred yards west, beeves still poured over the wire like turtles off a log. Turning in the saddle, he looked down the row of posts to the east and abruptly longed to follow it all the way to the Gulf Coast and that hardscrabble farm near Master Young's plantation. She was there right now, shaken by the reports that had trickled back from the Red River. His sweet Vennie had heard all about it—the killing, the theft, the flight. She had listened and denied and grieved, and in the end this ebony daughter of one of Master Young's sharecroppers had come to doubt everything Zeke had told her: his promise to return, his plans for the two of them, even his very love.

If he could just see her and look into those dark eyes and whisper the truth . . . if only. . . .

With a choking sob and a sting in his eyes, Zeke realized he could never go back.

Never.

Not when a hangman's rope would be waiting for him, that and the kind of hatred he could never bear to see in Vennie's eyes.

Zeke hadn't cried since he had been nine and pneumonia had taken from him the only parent he had ever known. But now his future seemed so formless, so empty and meaningless, that it was all he could do to contain his emotions. Alone in this frigid backcountry where there was nothing between him and the north pole but barbed wire, he had no reason to deny himself emotional release.

That is, except for one.

He was a cowboy.

Time and again in the saddle, Zeke had met with trying situations without blinking, but facing death was so much easier than facing what was inside him. How could he fight something he couldn't touch?

Zeke must have been in reverie for several minutes, for at a hail from behind he turned to see the other four cowhands approaching on horseback along the opposite side of the fence. They all rode with humps in their backs from cold, and the brims of their hats were dusted with snow.

"You made it," Will said quietly. There was something in his eyes—a hesitancy maybe, or a dilemma playing itself out—that had been there ever since Zeke had started to cut him out of that barbed wire.

"I wouldn't have bet a Rebel dollar on your chances, boy," said Hyler.

"*Mon Dieu!*" exclaimed Arch. "I venture to say that a trick rider I once saw in Paris could have taken lessons."

"Paris, my eye," grumbled Wampus doubtfully. "And anyhow, took a lot more skill what we done, workin' our way out 'fore we even hit the river."

"Blind luck on our part, pure and simple," admitted a still-subdued Will.

"Like hell," contended Wampus. "Any half-decent hand could've done what he did. Guaran-damn-tee it."

With a grin, Arch glanced at Wampus and then scanned the other faces. "A guarantee, indeed! I'm wont to guarantee that we couldn't coax fair

Wampus here into joining that herd again for a display of those extraordinary skills of his."

It took only a sharp breath from Hyler and a tightening of his already set jaw to end the augering. Again, Zeke was relieved; he wished he could stop finding himself the silent center of an argument.

"We've got enough riding to do," said Hyler, in case anyone misinterpreted. "We haven't found a Slash Five cow yet."

4

They trailed east along the fence line, the four Slash Five riders on one side, and the Negro day worker on the other. Will endured a couple of brutal miles, shivering all the way in a northeast wind that wouldn't quit, before Hyler pointed ahead to eight or ten cows standing beside a fence post.

Even at a distance, Will could see a Slash Five burned on their hips. But there was something strange about the beeves, the way the snow collected along their backbones as they apparently huddled for mutual warmth. The cows were almost statue-like, not a muscle twitching as the frightful blast ruffled their winter coats.

As Will approached within twenty yards and saw glassy eyes staring back, he understood all too well. Just as Zeke had said, the animals had frozen to death standing up.

If there was anything that struck a nerve in a cowboy, it was to find dead cattle for which he had been responsible. It didn't matter that he had no claim to ownership; an owner invariably would have abandoned a threatened herd long before most of his six-bits-a-day employees would have even considered it. A bovine was what made a cowboy a cowboy, with the help of a horse, and to lose one that bore his outfit's brand meant that he had failed.

A quiet curse hung in Will's throat as the five men reined up beside these monuments to winter's might. He half-expected Arch to needle Wampus about his earlier scoffing, but when Will glanced at Arch, he found the same solemn expression that Hyler wore.

"It looks bad, boys," said Hyler. "Really bad, I want to tell you."

He took his mount around the standing carcasses and started on down the fence line, and Will fell into the deepening set of tracks cut by his mount.

They rode on, rocked by first one gust and then another. Will did his best to shield his face by tilting head and hat into his shoulder, but wind or no wind, the cold was always there, watering his eyes, numbing his cheeks. The bridge of his nose suffered most, an intense ache that never went away, but almost as troubling were his hands, a pair of unfeeling clubs behind leather gloves.

Will didn't know anything about frostbite or hypothermia, but he didn't need a doctor to tell him that a wrong decision or two in this blizzard would earn a man his own place among those frozen cattle. Still, the snow had cast an evil beauty over this rugged country, softening the sharp rocks and hiding the dismal grays of winter grass. Even the cacti had a harsh appeal, the spiny pads of prickly pear catching flakes and the ordinarily dull green of tasajillo stalks assuming a more favorable hue against the white background.

Half a mile farther, just as they neared a rise, they came upon a break in the fence. For forty yards the posts had been leveled, the barbed wire, sometimes standing in coils, thrown out to either side of a beaten trail that bore south. In mid-break lay the carcass of a horse, but the animal had been so trampled that Will didn't recognize what was left of his own roan and saddle until he was almost upon them.

But there was more to the story. Three cattle carcasses, one on this side of the line and two more on the other, also marked the trail, and all three carried a Slash Five brand.

As Will and the others pulled rein, Hyler fixed crow's-feet eyes down the trace to the south. "I guess we've found our cows, boys. Found them or lost them, one."

"Wasn't us lost 'em," snapped Wampus, looking at the dead roan.

Will appreciated Hyler keeping his thoughts about the horse to himself, even though he knew about the accident. But Will didn't need anyone to tell him that he could have done better. His wreck had snapped the two lower strands and weakened the fence. Shaken, bleeding, facing a storm—what had any of that mattered? When he had run away from home at thirteen, carrying a burden no thirteen-year-old should have to, he had found in cowboying a way to bury all the memories in the kind of hard work and dedication in which a man could take pride. He had never shirked a duty, so why the hell had he yesterday in regard to that fence and not even given it a moment's thought since? There could be only one reason, one place to lay blame for yanking him out of a cowboy's world and drawing him back to that fiery night near Texarkana.

With resentment that bordered on hatred, Will turned to the Negro.

But Zeke had brought his Appaloosa through the gap in the fence and reined up before Hyler.

"Wasn't Mister Will's fault, I wants you to know. Still mighty stout, them top two strands was."

Will sure didn't feel worthy of a defense, but he was surprised beyond words that it was Zeke who gave it. Strangely, however, the unexpected support just made his guilt about so many things that much worse.

"Four strands would've been a hell of a lot stouter," argued Wampus. "Any greenhorn would've knowed to fix—"

"I'm honored to be in the presence of such an authority, Professor Wampus," interrupted Arch.

Will wasn't about to lie to himself any more than he already had all these years.

"Quit it, Arch." And then to Hyler, "Nobody to blame but me, Major. I want you to hear it straight from me."

He wanted to make eye contact with the older man in order to read any thoughts he might not vocalize, but the ranch manager was already studying the beaten course leading on through the snow.

"Breaking through may be all that saved them," said Hyler. "They might be standing here stiff as boards too if they hadn't."

"Going to be a particularly eventful roundup next spring if our noble bovines scatter all the way to Devils River," said Arch. "We'll certainly incur some attractive blisters on our buttocks."

"We will if we don't overtake them now," said Hyler. "Snow never lasts long here. When this thing blows itself out this afternoon and we've caught up, the five of us can turn them back."

Suffering under the icy wind, Will wasn't so certain, but at least the mere sprinkle of snow in the tracks was encouraging.

"Looks of things, can't be that far ahead," he said.

Taking the initiative, as he knew he should, Will reined his horse through the opening and started after the Slash Five herd. He didn't look to see if the others followed, but he could tell all he needed by the rattle of spurs and creak of saddles.

In mid-morning, that same freight train rumble and bawling chorus rose up from behind as another wave of cattle neared. Reining up, Will looked back past the trailing riders. Snow flurries hid the distance, but he knew what was there. The five of them had narrowly escaped before, but he knew they better not depend on luck again.

The others had halted as well, the snow-laden currents whipping in and out of their bent figures as they looked back.

"Comin' at us again, boys!" shouted Hyler.

"Damned if I don't concur," said Arch.

"Where in Sam Hill you been takin' us?" Wampus demanded of Will. "A blind goat could've done better. Just determined to get somebody killed, ain't you?"

Will knew they didn't have time to bicker, not with tons of beef-on-the-hoof bearing down out of the ghostly distance.

"Anybody got a fix on them?" he asked.

"Newton would have to sit under that apple tree a mite longer to decipher this one," said Arch.

"What the hell's apples got to do with any-thing!" snapped Wampus. "You damned idiot!"

Wampus was panicking, all right, but Will's pulse hammered as well. If they didn't take quick and decisive action, shallow graves would be a lot closer than he wanted to think. Only one of them was seasoned in dealing with the whims of migrating cattle, even if his experience had been like that of a man caught up in treacherous rapids.

"Zeke," Will forced himself to ask, "What do we got to do?"

"Stay out front, Mister Will. Just don't let 'em catch us."

Out of a snowy haze a hundred yards away, an entire army exploded. There were horns and hides and crushing hoofs, a charging line swallowing everything Will could see from left to right. He wasn't a military man, but he couldn't imagine an advancing battlefront more awesome.

"Got to ride!" he yelled, wheeling his horse and spurring it into flight.

As his bay achieved a gallop, he glanced back to find fast on his animal's hindquarters the other riders—Hyler working his spurs and Wampus flailing a quirt, a forward-leaning Arch urging his mount on with the king's English and a neck-hugging Zeke doing the same in a dialect no king would have understood.

A race between running horses and trotting beeves should have been no race at all, especially when the Slash Five herd had already cut a trail through the snow for the ponies. But fresh snow

now covered much of the trace, certainly well enough to hide the pitfalls that could bring a horse down: an armadillo burrow or prairie dog mound, even a loose rock or a knotty mesquite stump. Horse falls were a way of life for a cowboy—Will had proven that only yesterday—but to go down in front of a storming herd would be surefire tragedy today.

But there was something else that worried Will about this contest: When would it be over? Would he and the others get enough of a lead to feel secure in veering across the beeves' course, when visibility was so limited that none of them could even guess at the herd's breadth?

One thing was certain. In conditions like this, a rider better not overtax his horse for long, because a man set afoot might as well be face-up in a three-by-six.

After a couple of minutes of hard riding and harder thinking, Will did the prudent thing and eased his bay into a jog-trot. As they overtook him on either side, Hyler, Arch, and Wampus did the same with their mounts, but when Will looked back he found that Zeke had already relaxed the Appaloosa's gait and now trailed by fifty yards. No matter the bad feelings the Negro stirred in him, Will had to admit Zeke's wisdom when it came to a horse.

The migrating longhorns had disappeared into the white veil again, but the low hum and collective bellowing were ever-present reminders that they were still there.

"Few minutes ahead now, I reckon," offered Will.

"You 'bout rode our horses into the ground," complained Wampus. "Any damned fool oughta know better."

If Will could have flushed hot, he would have. "Didn't see nobody quirtin' that bronc but you."

"If complaints were dollars, gentlemen," interjected Arch, "our man Wampus would be a millionaire."

While Arch and Wampus jawed at one another, Will turned to Hyler. "Major, you really figure on this storm blowin' itself out come afternoon?"

The older man had pulled a red-checkered bandana up across his face, muffling his words a little. "Already warming up some, wouldn't you say?"

It was true that with the wind at his back, Will wasn't suffering the way he had earlier. But with his fingers, toes, and cheeks as numb as they were, how could he tell?

"I know you're manager and all," he said through chattering teeth, "but I'll tell you, I'm a little leery of this."

"This country's always hell on horses and women," said Hyler. "Especially women."

"Not much better on us. Maybe I could stand

it better if I had the right one keepin' the home fires burnin'."

A darkness seemed to sweep over Hyler's eyes. "I had that once and let it get away. Burying one wife already, I don't deserve another one."

Will was surprised at this unexpected insight into Hyler's character. "I never knowed you was married, Major. You talk like somethin' was your fault."

"It was. She had a fever when I went off. The war, sixty-four. I was rotating in and out of the militia, chasing deserters. A blizzard like this came on, and she was too sick to get wood. The fire burned down and she kicked the covers off and died. If I'd stayed at home, it never would have happened."

By the emotion in Hyler's voice, Will could only imagine the pain hidden by the bandana.

"Didn't have a choice, I guess," Will finally managed. "Had your duty."

"Duty!" The word came quickly, powerfully, almost like a curse. "Duty's what got my Elizabeth killed!"

As the ranch manager kicked his roan into a lope and surged ahead, Will couldn't help but wonder if death was exactly what blessed duty would net all of them in this blizzard from hell.

They forged on into noon and beyond, five fragile figures testing the limits of not only a cowhand's responsibility, but his very endurance.

They alternated their horses' gaits between a distance-eating jog-trot and a walk, dictated by the rumble of the ever-advancing herd behind. With every mile Will grew colder, increasingly numb, more concerned. The weather showed no sign of abating; if anything, the storm increased in intensity, dumping a dry, powdery snow until the trail of the Slash Five herd was only a suggestion ahead.

As they slowed their animals yet again, Will looked at Hyler and found him shivering. But the squinting eyes between hat brim and bandana still seemed to burn with determination, and Will couldn't help but ponder if all of this was somehow Hyler's way of kicking off his own covers so he could join Elizabeth.

"Major," said Will, reining up. His lips and tongue were so cold that he could barely form the word. "You've got to listen to me, Major."

Everyone must have read the seriousness in his voice, for four hunched forms suddenly were holding their mounts and facing him, their exposed features starting to take on the pallor of dead men.

"We can't go on like this," continued Will. "We just can't."

"So it's cattle be damned?" Hyler challenged.

"It's not that. It's not that at all. They're goin' to be fendin' for themselves, like they're doin' now. We got to do the same."

"I dare admit Will has a point," spoke up Arch. "Our bovines will be basking on the sunny Devils until song birds herald another roundup next spring."

Hyler scanned the terrible wilderness ahead. Tucking a gloved hand under his arm, he began rubbing it across his armpit. It was clear that his fingers were as frigid as Will's.

"I don't know." Hyler's quiet voice seemed only for himself. "Maybe I'll just go on alone awhile."

"You don't want to do that, Mister Major," said Zeke. "You sure don't."

Hyler turned quickly, anger flashing in his eyes. "Since when do I take advice from the likes of you?"

Taken aback, Will could only look at a white man and a Negro staring at one another. It was Zeke who lowered his gaze.

"*I* sure as hell ain't got no hold on you," interjected Wampus, making his own opinion clear with a glance back to the north.

Given Hyler's reaction to the Negro, Will was almost afraid to say what he knew he should. But he did.

"Major, we got a good lead on those cows behind us now. Why don't we try circlin' back around them, head for that stove?"

Hyler looked at him and breathed sharply. "I've got some cows to chase down."

Reining his horse into the fading trail of the Slash Five herd, the ranch manager once more urged his animal into as near a trot as the deepening snow would allow.

A little stunned, Will sat watching him recede into the flurries.

"What is it we're to do, Arch?" he finally asked, wishing that someone would tell him. "What's your book-learnin' say in times like this?"

But it was somebody who likely couldn't even read a book who answered.

"We's lookin' at a good man," said Zeke, his focus on the departing rider. "I be goin' with him."

Will didn't know which surprised him more, the obsession that had seemingly taken hold of Hyler or the Negro's unexpected loyalty. As Zeke started his Appaloosa after the troubled man, Will exchanged glances with the other two hands and listened to the warning of an inner voice.

"I don't like the looks of things, Arch," he said. "I sure as hell don't."

"I ain't no damned fool," said Wampus. "I'm startin' back if somebody will go with me."

"Nobody got a loop on you," Will said impatiently. "What about you, Arch?"

Arch seemed intent on sorting things out analytically as he shifted his eyes between Will, the concealed north horizon, and the two horsemen pulling away to the south.

"The major's been a prince of a man," he concluded. "I must say I'm not prone to deserting him. But Will, you cast the deciding ballot and I'll abide by it."

Will wished that Arch hadn't added to his already swelling burden, not when their lives could be at stake. But damn it, Arch was right. Giving up on cows was one thing, but giving up on a fellow hand or two was something a cowboy just didn't do.

With that inner voice warning *No! No!* Will turned his horse into the fresh tracks bearing south, and Arch and Wampus went with him.

5

They rode for another hour, the building snow forcing their horses to mere walks. With an unceasing wind pushing from behind and the packed snow ahead pushing back just as hard with every pace, Zeke knew this whole venture was an ordeal on more than just the figures in the saddle. The only encouraging development was that the hum of the migrating herd behind had shifted to the hidden west, suggesting that he and the other hands were no longer in its path.

Zeke had never been so cold. His very teeth ached to every gust that gnawed away not only at his willpower, but at his very fiber. Still, he refused to turn back, not just because facing the wind would increase his misery, but because Major Hyler pressed on without hesitation.

Zeke knew a good man when he saw one. After all, he had worked and ridden for Master Young his whole life. He knew the look in a good man's eyes and the tenor of one's voice, even if the major had made clear a Negro's place. If the two of them ever got out of this alive, maybe the major would come to respect his opinion just as Master Young had.

But the only sure thing right now was how grim their situation was. As far as they had come in these deteriorating conditions, they were fast approaching the point of no return—the point at which they could never turn back and have any hope of reaching the line shack before dark. Zeke had come to accept that this storm already had its teeth so deep in this land that there was no chance of it letting go anytime soon, and he couldn't even imagine the horrors of spending a night in it.

Still, he wouldn't broach the matter out loud, not after the major had silenced him earlier. But he wasn't sorry when the mysterious cowhand named Will held up his hand in a signal to stop and everyone heeded it.

For tense moments, Will's head was down, as if he was gathering his thoughts, but the moment the Slash Five cowhand faced Hyler, Zeke knew what he would say.

"More than half the day's gone, Major, and there's not a Slash Five heifer in sight. Right here's where we got to turn around."

"What I been tellin' these idiots, Major, ever since them cattle got off our tail," grumbled Wampus.

"Dark certainly would not be our ally in these conditions," agreed Arch.

In the ranch manager's eyes, Zeke could read the tension of an unbroken bronc feeling the draw of its first cinch. Will, obviously uncomfortable under Hyler's prolonged stare, glanced down and shook his head.

"They're just cows," said Will. "It's not like they're some—some woman. Come on, let's head back in to a fire and some coffee."

"That's what I say," joined in Wampus. "Heifers and woman be damned—let 'em all go to hell."

As though gouged by spurs, Hyler whirled on Wampus. The two men sat their mounts several yards apart, but the distance closed quickly as the major seized his quirt and spurred his horse for the cowhand. Hyler never pulled rein, driving eight hundred pounds of muscled bronc broadside into Wampus's sorrel, staggering it.

Suddenly the major's quirt was flashing, the leather braids striking a startled and cowering Wampus in the ribs, the shoulder, the neck. Only an arm thrown up in instinctive defense and the shying of his horse kept the lashes from his stunned face.

"What the hell! What the hell!"

It was all that Wampus could manage as the scourging persisted, and Zeke wondered what the cowhand had done to merit a runaway slave's punishment.

Suddenly Will's bay was between the two. "He

didn't mean nothin' by it, Major! That's just Wampus!"

Still enraged like someone possessed, Hyler seemed unable for a moment to distinguish Will from Wampus, and the quirt almost fell on the wrong man before the major caught himself. But his eyes stayed wild and his breaths frenzied as he glared back and forth between Will and a retreating Wampus. Finally, with a nod to Will, Hyler started away into the snows of a wilderness that stretched on before him all the way to the Devils River.

"Crazy SOB!" cried Wampus, still wincing as he felt his neck. "What the hell's the matter with him?"

Will took his horse abreast of Wampus and peeled back his collar. "Coat took most of it. Never did know when to keep your mouth shut."

With Hyler out of earshot, Arch drew near the pair. "I perceive you have insight that eludes me, Will."

Will turned, making eye contact, and then looked over Arch's shoulder at Hyler receding into the flurries.

"I don't know, Arch, but I think he's all shook up about his wife."

"His wife?"

"You and Wampus was busy augerin' back up-trail and don't guess you was listenin'. Lost her durin' the war. Blames himself for bein' gone and her takin' sick and freezin' to death."

"What the hell's that got to do with things?" asked Wampus. "Why the hell—"

"Arch, you got the education," Will continued. "Any way you think all this weather's triggered somethin' in him? Could he be out there lookin' to die same way she done?"

"Major impressed me as behaving peculiar ever since the two of us departed headquarters this morning. He's always seemed to exude loneli-ness—something in his eyes if you ever catch him unawares. But when we rode out from headquarters, he kept looking back and whispering something like 'Liz-beth . . . Liz-beth.' "

"That was her, Arch. That was his wife he was leavin' behind to die all over again."

During the exchange, Zeke had taken his horse closer to hear the words over the wind. To insert himself into the conversation might be to risk rebuke again, but he went ahead and did so anyway.

"Maybe he got the madness. When I was a young'n, drivin' them mossy-horns Kansas way, a man took the madness and went after the cocinero with a ax. We tied him to the wagon wheel, but we done left him too much slack. Poor man, he hung hisself while we was sleepin'."

"The human mind reins supreme as a mystery," said Arch, "and the four of us aren't likely to solve it perched on our horses in a blizzard. Our paramount concern right now is not the why, but the what."

"As in, what in hell are we doin' now," completed Will, lowering his head dejectedly.

"I say leave the SOB!" growled Wampus. "Treat him like a mad dog!"

"That's the man give you a job," reminded Will.

"Yeah? Same man as give me a horse whippin', too."

Zeke looked back at Hyler growing fainter in the blowing snow. One thing was sunlight clear, even in a storm like this—the major was not going to turn back willingly, even if it cost him his life.

"If Mister Major was a outlaw horse," he posed, "we'd put the loop on him and drag him back."

Will looked at Arch, and Arch looked back at Will.

"This is goin' to get ugly, Arch," said the latter.

"I know it is, Will."

"Ugly, hell!" exclaimed Wampus. "You go playin' with the crazy fool and we's all gonna die out here."

Zeke again studied Hyler's vanishing form and reached his own decision. One good man was already dead because of him, and he wouldn't let another meet the same fate even if it meant risking everything. Suddenly Zeke again had reason for being.

"Arch, you thinkin' like me, aren't you," said Will. "That we got to do whatever we have to to bring him back."

When Zeke turned back to the Slash Five hands, he saw Arch's chest rising as if steeling himself for what was to come.

"Anything," said Arch, "is more humane than letting a disturbed man wander off in such conditions."

"All right," said Will, "it's you and me then."

Zeke reached for the tie string of his catch-rope. "I just passin' through, but I do what I can."

"You all can go freeze in hell if you're a mind," snapped Wampus, starting back to the north. "I'm through with this."

"You do what you got to," said Will impatiently. He reined his horse into the tracks of Hyler's mount. "Let's go, y'all, before we lose him."

It took brutal minutes, but the three of them overtook Hyler and surrounded him just as they had planned: Will close on the left, Arch hard on the right, and Zeke in behind Hyler's roan with loop already in hand. They held the formation for so long that Zeke wondered if the Slash Five riders would ever take action, and then Will broke the anxious silence.

"Major, I'm askin' you one last time to turn back with us."

Even from Zeke's vantage point in rear, it was

71

clear that the major's head never tilted an inch in Will's direction.

"You got to answer me, Major," Will pressed.

Still, Hyler's hat remained pointed into the gathering snows ahead, but at least this time he spoke.

"I already told you my answer."

Will looked back and gave Zeke the pre-arranged signal, a nod. Zeke swung his loop a couple of times, and it darted out like the strike of a rattler and settled over the major. To Zeke's yank and dally, the lariat snapped tight and pinioned Hyler's arms to his ribs. At the same instant, Will seized the cheek of the roan's bridle, preventing the animal from bolting, while Arch clutched the major to keep him from falling out of the saddle.

"The hell!"

Hyler had more to say, a lot more, for although the lariat might truss him like a calf at a branding fire, it could do nothing to bind his tongue. The major unleashed a torrent of invectives so personally damning against Will and Arch that Zeke felt as sympathetic toward them as he did Hyler.

"Major, you got to settle down!" pleaded Will. "You're just not thinkin' straight!"

Still the venom spewed, and Hyler worked his boot out of the stirrup and drove it into Will's thigh with such force that it made the latter man's horse shy. Will lost his hold on the bridle, but he immediately lunged and seized the reins, which allowed him to back away enough to avoid Hyler's continued kicks.

Now the major turned his attention to the cowhand at his right, but Arch had his horse flush against the roan so that Hyler couldn't extricate his boot, much less use it as a weapon. Still, a man driven to extremes wasn't afraid to resort to measures just as extreme. Even though Arch's arm about his shoulders was intended to steady rather than restrain, Hyler tried to fight him away by repeatedly throwing his head into Arch's ribs and neck.

Zeke had only one play to protect both men and he took it. He backed the Appaloosa and, by means of the rope, dragged the ranch manager out of the saddle.

"You'll break his neck!" protested Will.

But Zeke had already considered the consequences and knew the snow would cushion his fall. Still, any wreck was hard on a man of Hyler's age, and as his shoulder slammed down between the shifting hoofs, he seemed to lose all his wind.

Will was off his animal quickly. "Keep the horses off of him!"

Then he was at Hyler's side, shielding the gasping man from the boogered roan.

Guilt swept over Zeke in a way that it hadn't

since Master Young had collapsed. Immediately he took his horse closer, relaxing the rope.

"I sure sorry, Mister Major. Awful sorry."

Will spun as he began loosening the loop from Hyler's chest. "What the hell give you the right?"

"His intent was merely to restrain Major from himself, Will," spoke up Arch. "The same as you and I."

"Didn't have to do it that way!" contended Will, working the loop off Hyler's shoulders.

He continued to rail under his breath as he slipped a supporting hand under the major's head and brushed snow from his face.

"Major, you hearin' me?"

Hyler regained both breath and fight at the same moment. "I'm firing every last one of you!"

"You do what you got to," said Will. "That's just what we're doin'. Let's get you on your horse and turn around for camp."

"I wouldn't cross the street with the likes of you!" said Hyler, but he went ahead and let Will help him to a sitting position.

Nevertheless, no sooner had the major struggled to his feet than he took a swing at Will—a short, crisp blow that caught the unsuspecting cowhand in the mouth.

Will staggered back, blood oozing from his lip. "Damn it, Major!" He wagged his head angrily, slinging red droplets. "Just tryin' to help you!"

"You call dragging me off my horse helping

me? I'll see the three of you up for assault!"

Will bent over, trying to stifle the flow of blood with a hand to his lip. "You do that, Major. We'll go hole up in the line shack, and when the weather breaks the four of us can ride in to the sheriff at San Angelo and settle matters."

"Will I have to add kidnapping to the counts? That's just what it would be!"

Suddenly Zeke wished he'd never had any part of this. Once the law was brought in, the charges wouldn't stop with assault or even kidnapping. There would also be Master Young's killing. Even if he wasn't lynched by a mob, the result would be the same—rope fibers burning his neck as his boot heels clicked together.

Arch led Hyler's roan up and positioned it so the manager could gain the stirrup.

"Step up, Major," he urged. "Before long we'll be thawing before a stove and dining on warm airtights."

Zeke didn't like the look the major flashed Arch, but at least he climbed stiffly into the saddle with an assist from Will. For a moment, Arch continued to deny him the reins.

"May I trust you with these?" he asked.

Hyler breathed sharply and reached. Hesitantly, Arch gave up his grip.

"The pits of hell with you!"

Simultaneous with the cry, Hyler spun the roan and spurred it away to the south.

6

When a man's own life might be on the line, where did his responsibility to someone else end?

As Will grabbed the saddle horn and threw his leg across his horse, he asked himself that and more. Every additional minute they spent chasing Hyler was another sixty seconds they wouldn't have to get back to line camp before dark. He had a terrible decision to make, and no time left to make it.

"We've no choice, Will," said Arch as Hyler receded into flurries suddenly growing heavier. "We can retreat with honor now and perhaps hope for line camp by dark-thirty."

Will watched the snows swallowing the major. "I-I don't like this, Arch. Leavin' a man to—"

"Let him be, Will. Turn around with honor and allow that good man out there one last measure of dignity."

Will would never know what his decision would have been, for suddenly the wind began to rage, frightening in its shriek and even more terrifying in the way its snow-heavy currents blinded and knifed through his clothes. A man simply couldn't endure it, but here he was, astride a horse in a wilderness turned whiteout, a helpless figure suspended in an abrupt purgatory. Even the storm's onslaught the day before had been tame by comparison.

Will's horse shied, and all of a sudden he was completely disoriented. His only frame of reference was the saddle beneath him, and although he called out for the others, he couldn't hear his own voice. He was alone, for all intents and purposes, a scared man facing something he knew he couldn't lick.

It was a cowboy's instinct, when all else failed, to fall back on the animal that made him what he was. He gave the bay its head and felt it begin to drift with the unbearable wind. The flames in the Texarkana night surged through his mind, and he thought how ironic that his judgment came in the form of numbing cold rather than boiling fire. Once again, the old regrets ripped at his heart. He could have questioned his father as they had approached the shack with those sloshing buckets. He could have pleaded with him to reconsider as they had mounted the sagging porch. Hell, he could have cried out a ten-year-old's warning to the family inside before a match ever ignited in the darkest night Will had ever known.

Good God, what right had he to live to

manhood, denying as he had that very chance to so many children? Their bones, raked from the ashes, had cried out from a mass grave all these years, and he had been uncaring enough to pretend that none of it had ever happened.

Damn him! He deserved death—and worse! Just let him die and get it over with!

While Will relived and regretted and hated, the bay continued to drift. Minutes went by, or maybe hours; in this nightmare of penance, there was no way to tell. He had never realized that broad daylight could turn so dark, except in a sandstorm, and he would have believed night had already overtaken him if not for a strange twilight that never went away. Still, a horse's innate night vision was of no benefit in these conditions, and repeatedly Will felt the drag of packed snow against his boots as the animal plowed through belly-deep drifts.

Will didn't know the signs of hypothermia or frostbite, but troubling things were happening to his body. Shivering wasn't foreign to him, but this was an intense quake that robbed him of strength. He believed the reins were still loose in his glove, but his sense of touch could neither assure nor deny. When he searched for the horn he had difficulty closing his hand around it, much less maintaining a grip.

He was fast losing coordination, and if he'd had his wits about him he would have feared tumbling off into the snow. The truth was, the cold preyed just as brutally on his mental faculties, to the point that a curious apathy gave way to a strange euphoria.

The comforting whorls of ice dancing in the twilight . . . a strange warmth burning its way up from deep in his fiber . . . the effortless glide that carried him nearer and nearer a nether world ready to welcome. . . . All these things urged him to close his eyes and let the inevitable take its course all the way into eternity.

But one thing wouldn't let him. He seemed drawn yet again across years and miles to that razing fire, only this time he wasn't merely looking on and shuddering. He was trapped inside with all those he had damned to choking screams and burning lungs, feeling for himself a small measure of the engulfing flames that tortured before killing. And Will knew that no one who had played a role in that horrid night deserved anything less than an end just as cruel.

With self-hatred alone, Will fought back against his euphoria. Let him die, all right, but not here, not now, not when he couldn't know the same degree of pain and fear.

He felt his horse unaccountably shy, and then something bumped his right foot just before he flinched to a sharp prod in his opposite thigh. About him rose up the muffled bellowing of cattle, the kind of thing that could rouse a cowboy from a feet-first trip to the cemetery. Abruptly he was back, alert and suffering and scared, and equally secure in the knowledge that he would pay his dues before this was over.

A herd had swept him up again, unseen horns hooking his legs as his pony rocked to the impact of powerful bodies just as hidden. The very flurries seemed alive, a surging current carrying horse and rider along a decidedly curving course. It was less an animated tide than a whirlpool of muscled beeves and irrepressible horn, and Will realized that this was more than the flight of a migrating herd. It was a mill, an instinctive defense against extreme conditions.

As the beeves spiraled in on themselves, the perpetual motion and tightly packed bodies would generate heat and shield against the wind. Even from the higher vantage point of a saddle, Will already felt the first degree of warmth since he had huddled around the line-shack stove that morning. Over the years, he had chased down his share of runaway beeves and forced them into herd-saving mills treacherous to riders, but he had never figured that one day he would welcome this frenzy of sparring horns and bruising swipes.

If his horse could just avoid an intestine-spilling hooking . . . if his bay could only gouge out room for its wiry legs to keep pace . . . if both of them could just match the endurance of longhorns so known for hardiness . . .

Any way Will added it up, that was an awfully lot of *ifs* to hope for.

The minutes passed like hours, or maybe they were—hours of fear and panic and anticipated death. At least this was more like it, a lingering scourging at once physical, mental, and psychological. He had every second of it coming to him, but to give the one life he had for the six he had taken could never be more than a down payment. The rest, he figured, would have to wait until hell.

Will already knew what the place looked like. Ribbons of fire leaping against the Texarkana midnight. Boiling smoke shrouding uncaring stars. An inferno lapping corpses already charred beyond recognition. He wondered if hell would ever end, or if he would be damned to punishment until the sun itself burned out.

Will had never analyzed the dynamics of a mill, but he knew that its currents funneled animals from outside to center and back out again in relentless cycle. Whiteout or not, he could always judge his location by dramatic shifts in temperature and wind strength. There must have been thousands of beeves, considering the length of time between extremes, and he cringed at what would happen if an animal ahead gave in to exhaustion and fell. His bay was already ridden down, and for it to negotiate a sprawled carcass in all the mad shoving was too much for any rider to expect, damned or not.

The whiteout finally relented about the time Will's faltering horse cycled outside again, and he reached a decision that could either save his life or ensure his death. Undisturbed snow lay only three rampaging lines of beeves away, and he cut the bay toward it. He bumped a steer hard, only to be repelled. He tried a second time and a third and gained a place in the adjacent line. He repeated the process twice more, but it was a brutal fight against rangy muscle and slinging horns before he completely escaped the mill.

But now other factors had come into play. Even with increased visibility, he was still as turned around as ever. The afternoon had worn on, robbing him of any hope of reaching the line shack in daylight even had he known the way. Although the wind had lessened, that same penetrating cold remained, biding its time until temperatures would plummet by night to the point at which no man so exhausted could survive.

Will had to have fire or shelter, but the prospect of either on this snowy divide was unimaginably grim. He reined the bay into the wind in search, hoping that he was at least bearing in the general direction of camp.

He pushed on mechanically, the tilted brim of his hat guarding his features from the elements. Facing the wind was so much more numbing, and for the most part he rode with head down for the utmost protection. Every time he did look up, he found the same thing—frozen wasteland marked by snow-powdered prickly pear, tasajillo stalks, and occasional mesquites with limbs that drooped in a thick coat of ice.

Nightfall was almost on him when he rode upon a white-dusted packrat nest on the lee of deadfall that had once been a sizable mesquite. The limbs, spidery and gnarled, shielded the den of small sticks from the blowing snow and nurtured a waist-high drift on the stump's windy side.

Desperate times called for desperate measures, and Will couldn't imagine a situation more urgent. As he pulled rein, he checked his shirt pocket for the muslin sack that held tobacco, cigarette papers, and, most importantly, matches. Taking up his catch-rope, which was tied hard and fast around the horn, he began trying to dismount.

He knew it wouldn't be easy for a man frozen to the saddle. His first step was to slide his hand under his thigh and lift his right boot out of the stirrup. Even so, he feared he might never swing his leg over the cantle, but by leaning in the opposite direction he managed to drag it across. Gravity did the rest, but he fell backward in the snow when he couldn't extricate his left boot from the stirrup.

Spent, he lay there, his toe still locked in place,

and reassured the bay with quiet words. Fortunately, the pony was too weak to bolt, but it was another anxious minute before he freed himself.

Will pulled himself up with the aid of the stirrup and inspected the den. Brushing away powdery snow, he found enough dry tinder inside to encourage him. Realizing he needed both hands, he played out the coil of rope and, with difficulty, secured his end to a nearby algerita bush.

But the real challenge came when Will removed his gloves and tried to untie the draw string of his muslin pouch. He just didn't have the dexterity, not in a merciless cold that took more and more from him with every minute. Finally resorting to his teeth, he opened the bag just enough to shake a few matches into his palm, along with rolling paper and a sprinkle of tobacco. The latter dispersed quickly in the wind, but he saved the papers by clamping one palm over the other.

He sat down in a controlled fall, catching himself with an elbow in the snow. He worked his clasped hands inside the nest, depositing items more valuable than gold, but retrieving his matches from the twisted sticks was another matter. They were so tantalizingly close—a fire, for God's sake, was so tantalizingly close—but all he could do was stir the matches with fingers that couldn't respond.

Will tried again and again, losing almost all hope until he withdrew a single match that had lodged precariously between stiff digits. He had it almost up to a waiting palm before the brush of a protruding stick stole it away.

This was torture, all right, the sort that someone of Will's ilk deserved. Still, he refused to give up, and he retrieved and lost five more matches before he successfully transferred one to his palm. Now if he could only strike it as he had done so many times before.

But this wasn't like other times, when a failed attempt had meant a missed smoke or maybe a cold stove or supper. This was do or die, and he steeled his nerves before trying to position the match in his palm so he might ignite it. All he could do was push it along a lifeline growing ever shorter, but finally he had it in place at a forty-five degree angle in the fork of his fingers.

The head of a match was highly flammable, and usually all Will had to do was rasp his thumbnail across it. But with slabs of meat for hands, he just couldn't apply the proper force. Overwhelmed by frustration and panic, he made a last-ditch effort by dragging the head across bark, but the match only slipped away, burying itself in the under-lying maze.

Will wanted to cry. He would have cried, except that he was too dehydrated. He had given his all, and it hadn't been enough.

"I help you, I will."

Will whirled, finding a black face framed against a deadly white world. He had been so intent on starting a fire that he hadn't noticed Zeke's approach, but there he was, kneeling close, and behind him stood a horse staked to the same algerita bush as Will's.

"Fingers is plum' gone."

Will mouthed the words and sound came out, but with numb lips and chattering teeth, he wasn't sure if anything he said was intelligible.

"I do it," said Zeke. "I got to."

Will hadn't realized that Zeke had brought a war bag over from his saddle until the cowhand produced the makings for a smoke. Blocking the wind with his body, the Negro rolled a cigarette. It required a lot of effort, for his fingers didn't want to work either, but in the finished product Will saw only one more stroke of white in a land that didn't need any more.

Vaguely, Will realized that his own thinking wasn't what it should have been, but to watch a man waste his time on a smoke when the undertaker had them by the throat was more than he could take.

"What are you doin'?" he demanded.

But the cigarette was already in the corner of Zeke's mouth, and now he was trying repeatedly to ignite a match with his thumbnail.

"Said, what the hell you doin'!"

Suddenly a flame erupted in the dusk, enticing Zeke to lean into it with a cupped hand as he drew on the cigarette. The match quickly went out, but that didn't stop Will from reaching for it with a hand too far gone to grip it. As he looked, though, he saw a glow at cigarette's end and a puff of exhaled smoke that made Will half-laugh in derision. Here they were, damned near dead, and all the Negro could do was sit there drawing on that butt.

But maybe Zeke had something else in mind. Turning into the wind, he placed his face over the nest's opening and flicked the cigarette down among the matches and papers scattered in the sticks.

Will's hopes surged. Foolish, hell! This was somebody with enough smarts to give them a chance!

Peering inside, Will could see the cigarette burning among tinder reluctant to ignite, and then Zeke's hand was there as well, raking it closer and closer to the certain fire starter.

"Come on, little pill!" Zeke encouraged as the butt contacted a wad of papers. "Be the best smoke I ever had!"

"Give it some air!" cried Will. "Move—give it air!"

Zeke withdrew and Will hovered over it alone, blowing on it as gently as his numb lips would allow. The paper burst into flames, and then came the crack of an igniting match, and another and another. All of a sudden tongues of fire were rising through twisted sticks with almost feathery caresses.

"Keep goin'!" cried Will. "Just keep goin'!"

Then Zeke was there, adding twigs and blowing, and in another few seconds they had a blaze and warmth and real hope.

Will couldn't escape the irony as the crackling flames fought against the dark night.

A fire started by a Negro was saving the life of someone who by fire had taken the lives of an entire Negro family.

What justice was there in that? Or was the burden of realizing the irony a part of the punishment that would go with him all the way into yet another fire—hell itself?

Maybe dying alone in the cold would have been better after all.

"Feelin's startin' to come back, Mister Will. All exceptin' my feet."

They had dragged a sizable log before the fire and now sat side by side, but Will didn't acknowledge Zeke with even a glance. The truth was, Will's feet were more than numb. Through his boot leather they felt as hard as blocks of ice. He wasn't sure what that meant, but it couldn't be good.

"You the only one I seen," said Zeke. "Got a bad feelin' 'bout 'em all."

Will wished that it had been any of the others, even surly Wampus, who had stumbled upon him. He wished this bearer of so much judgment had been the one to wander off in the storm, maybe never to come back. He wished, but he also realized something.

Zeke had very likely saved his life twice now.

"Sorry you has to put up with the likes of me," Zeke added.

Now Will did look at him, finding the flicker of the fire in his features as the Negro stared into it.

"Snakebit, I is," Zeke continued, "and that rattler, he hides in my pocket and bites ever'body that comes around."

Will had his wishes, all right, but truth was truth.

"You didn't throw me in that bob-wire," he said quietly. "You didn't bring this storm up neither, or send Major chasin' after ghosts."

"I ain't so sure. I ain't so sure about you neither, Mister Will. You tolerates me, you stands up for me, but you' eyes fights with you'self."

Will flinched uncomfortably. Was he so transparent that an uneducated black man could see right through him?

"I don't remember askin' you," he muttered. Maybe he was an open tally book, but he damned sure didn't appreciate being sized up that way.

Zeke fell silent, and for a long while Will heard

90

only the pop of wood in flames that both saved and condemned.

"I fights with myself too," Zeke finally said. "I puts a good whippin' on me, and it ain't never enough."

Will wished he would shut up; nobody else could even begin to bear the load that was on his shoulders. Still, a question that sprang to mind found its way to his lips.

"So what call you got to have your insides twisted?"

The Negro's features went even darker. The scoring in his forehead deepened as well, and he shuddered and drew his ragged coat tighter around his shoulders.

"I done plenty I ashamed of," he whispered as his head sagged. "I can't never go back. My Vennie, she a-waitin' for me till she heard bad, and now I can't never go back."

All of a sudden Will wished that he could go back, back as far as that night nineteen years ago. Abruptly he felt a strange bond with this Negro —and fought against it the same moment.

Damn it, what was the matter with him? This was a colored man, for God's sake, someone who had reminded and tormented ever since Will had looked up from that slashing barbed wire and seen him.

"Guess there's things chase after ever'body," Will finally allowed.

Zeke seemed to digest that as he rose and pulled out more mesquite deadfall.

"My master, he'd have somethin' to say if he was here." Zeke laid the limbs across a blaze hungry for it. "He'd say, 'Zeke, ain't what's back yonder behind you, it's what's ahead-on that matters.' I can hear him plain like that fire a-poppin'. But I so busy lookin' back, I can barely sees around me, much less ahead-on."

The words may have been passed along by a Negro, but they cut straight to Will's situation. "Who's this master you're talkin' about?"

Zeke hesitated as if gathering his thoughts, but judging by the quake that entered his voice as he answered, he couldn't corral his emotions as easily.

"He was my master first, when I was a young'n workin' the fields near the big water. Then I got to be his ridin' fool, drivin' them mossy-horns from you-can-till-you-can't. He was my boss man then, but I still called him Master. Sure 'nough good man, he was."

"You say was."

"Yes, sir, he . . ." Zeke's face became a mask of regret and his voice dropped to a whisper, as if he were speaking only to himself. "He dead, sure is. He dead and I can't never go back."

"So him bein' dead's got somethin' to do with it?"

The wind shifted, and a dark cloud of smoke

fell over Zeke like dirt across a dead man's face. When it cleared a little, his wide eyes seemed scared, even lost, and his lips had begun to tremble. Will figured his own features hadn't looked much different from the moment he had first seen this ghost from his past.

"I . . . I can't never go back," the Negro whispered again.

"Well, I can't neither, Zeke. Maybe a lot of folks can't."

Acrid smoke suddenly choked Will and lingered in his throat, right alongside bitter residue that had endured for almost two decades now. He didn't know which of the two made his eyes begin to burn.

"So what's a-snappin' at you' heels, Mister Will?"

Will glanced down at quivering digits that still seemed to smell of kerosene. "More than I can ever get away from."

"Me and you, we's kinda alike, ain't we."

Abruptly Zeke seemed framed against the Texarkana flames.

"We're not nothin' alike."

The long-ago fire roared, flaring against the night.

"Sorry for sayin' different," said Zeke, "but you got the same look I sees ever' time I holds a lookin' glass. Like a man that's got the hants all around."

Right now, with the firelight making the surrounding gloom all the darker, the hants seemed awfully close to Will, and he couldn't keep from glancing over his shoulder.

"How . . . How's a man ever shake them?" he asked.

Zeke gave a sigh of resignation. "They's like a bad dream, they is. You wake up and think they's gone, but sooner or later you lay you' head down again and here they come. They just stay there with you—don't matter if you ride all the way from the Big Red."

Or from Texarkana, thought Will.

Abruptly the campfire lost all warmth, or Will the ability to feel it—either way a strange terror. He rose stiffly and staggered closer, but even as he stretched out his hand, the blaze seemed to retreat farther.

What the hell . . .

But maybe this already was perdition, a place where punishment came in ways a cowboy could never understand. Still, Will did what common sense told him and seized more dead-fall.

The limb was stubborn, buried in brush loathe to let go, but he tugged and twisted until the pile itself bucked like a green-broke bronc.

Suddenly a vibration like maracas chilled what little warm blood Will had left.

"Rattle-tail! Watch it, Mister Will!"

Something struck Will's leggings shin-high and he recoiled, his leg oddly burdened by a limb that wasn't a limb. He dragged it with him as he stumbled back and lost his footing, and when he fell the firelight painted a terrible picture of a rattlesnake with its fangs buried in his leggings.

Thawed ground slammed into Will's back and his boot flew up, throwing the four footer toward his face. He only had time to turn his head, but icy rattles still slapped him hard across the cheek.

Will glimpsed a silhouette moving against the blaze and Zeke came up with a flaming firebrand. Flashing one way and then another over Will's leg, it streamed sparks against the night.

"Git!" Zeke struck the snake a glancing blow. "Git off of there!"

Will didn't know what to do except let raw instinct take over. He thrashed and kicked, but the rattler clung fast, a demon straight out of the brimstone.

"Be still a minute, Mister Will! Be still!"

Still, hell! He had a rattler he couldn't shake!

But Zeke persisted with the plea, and frantic seconds later the Negro caught up with the diamondback and seized it behind the triangular head.

"Got you! Got you!" he exclaimed, yanking with such force that it lifted Will's leg.

"Get it off! Get—"

In mid-cry Will's leggings yielded and Zeke pulled away, the fangs neutralized by the clamp of his hand. As the rattler coiled around Zeke's arm, firelight played in a set of devil eyes as cold and piercing as anything Will had ever seen.

Zeke wheeled to the fire. "You be supper, mister rattle-tail."

Unfurling the snake from his elbow, he tossed it down among coals glowing orange.

Will came to his feet trembling and stared into the flames. Maybe Zeke was right. Maybe Zeke was snakebit, just as he said. Maybe all of those he touched took up his curse and made it their own.

Looking around and reading a lot more than flickering light in that ebony face, Will considered and shuddered.

8

When the rattlesnake stopped squirming in the fire, Zeke forked it out with a limb and set about skinning and dressing it with his pocketknife. Soon he and Will were roasting equal portions on sticks, and a few minutes later nourishing meat began to fill the hole in Zeke's belly.

The nearby melting snow proved just as essential, and with strength and hydration returning a little, the two men did as cowboys should and dragged the saddles off their jaded mounts. Zeke knew that he and Will had caught a break in stumbling on a place ready for fire, but so much still depended on the condition of their ponies.

For a while the cowhands sat back against their saddles, the horse blankets underneath for insulation, and kept the fire blazing. Will eventually dozed off, but Zeke held out, watching the lapping flames and considering a future that now had lost the direction granted so fleetingly by Major Hyler.

Zeke wondered what Vennie was doing this

night, whether she was lying awake and dwelling on her hatred for him, or if she was already sleeping carefree in another man's arms. Zeke didn't know which image hurt worse, but either was enough to crush any hope for tomorrow.

Master Young, as well, was never far from Zeke's thoughts, and on this night, fresh after he had spoken of this good man, Young almost seemed to warm his hands before the same blaze. Zeke pondered what his onetime master had thought in those final moments, if he'd had time to grasp Zeke's role in the incident. Would Master Young hold it against him if they met up on some far-off shore? Or did the Almighty Himself not even understand, or at least not enough to keep him out of those everlasting fires?

Zeke never knew when he fell asleep, but when he awoke it was dawn and the fire was down to coals. A solid night's rest had refreshed him and brightened his outlook, especially considering that the sky was clear and the wind no longer was as fierce. Nevertheless, his frozen feet told him that a lot of challenges lay ahead.

Will was still asleep, his saddle for a pillow as he curled like a house cat, while the horses beyond stirred in the drifting smoke. The animals had gone without water or forage for more than twenty-four hours now, and Zeke could only hope that each could hold up under a couple of hundred pounds of rider and saddle.

He rose, wondering if feet that he couldn't even feel would still work. He swayed a little, but they seemed to hold him up all right. Hoisting the riding tack, he trudged through crunching snow and proceeded to bridle and saddle the Appaloosa. He was tightening the girt when he heard the rattle of a saddle behind, followed by a quick "Damn it!"

Turning, he found Will sprawled beside his rigging in the path that Zeke's boots had cut in the snow.

"You' feet like mine, Mister Will? They's there, but you wobble on 'em ever' step? I give you a hand?"

Will waved him off and struggled up with the clumsiness of a newborn foal. But bending over and straightening again with a saddle in tow demanded balance that Will just didn't have, and he fell a second time, a third.

Now Zeke didn't ask; staggering over, he took up the gear and then started for the bay without offering the man on all-fours a hand. A cowboy had a lot of pride, and Zeke wanted to leave him with as much self-respect as possible.

Even after Zeke saddled the bay for Will, though, he wasn't sure the Slash Five cowboy could mount up by himself. Indeed, even with a grip on the horn, Will searched in vain for the stirrup as his skittish horse pivoted repeatedly. Zeke, already in the saddle, finally brought his own horse abreast and held the bay in place. Still, Will had to use his hand to guide his boot through the stirrup before he could climb on.

With the sun rising across a glittering snow-field, Zeke finally had his bearings again. Line camp and that wood-burning stove seemed a lot closer now, but not close enough, considering the flesh-eating cold that struck him as he reined his horse to the north.

The Appaloosa cut a trace in the snow for the trailing bay and its bent rider, who had yet to say much this morning. Every time Zeke looked back, he found Will's face wrenched by pain. The cowhand rode with his jaw cupped in his hand, reminding Zeke of a time on the Arkansas when a bad tooth had dealt misery. Zeke had finally managed to pull it, but he wondered if Will's problem could be fixed so easily. For one thing, his face was swollen, and his skin had an ugly gray-white cast.

Zeke slowed the Appaloosa, allowing the bay to overtake it so that the men rode abreast.

"You hurtin' this mornin', Mister Will?"

Will kept his teeth close-set, rendering his delayed answer almost unintelligible. "Whole jaw's about to fall off."

"You all swelled up like a bloated cow. I think the cold got you."

"Never hurt so bad. Little wind there is kills me."

Zeke glanced toward the sun that hovered over the horizon; the frozen wasteland caught the rays and dispersed them like a thousand shiny knives.

"Ol' man in sky warm things up maybe," said Zeke, "but best we keep our hats low over our eyes."

Zeke had particular reason for concern. He didn't have much experience with snow, but he had worked in Master Young's cotton fields enough as a boy to respect the glare of an unrelenting sun. His eyes had been sensitive to light ever since he had hoed row after row without a hat one long season, and even though this early morning orb was at his side and his hat brim tilted down, he already squinted and dreaded.

But Will evidently hurt too much to worry about a little sunshine.

"Dog in this kind of misery," he whispered, "I'd shoot him. Damn sure."

"Maybe we's both payin' the Boss Man, we is."

"Pay who?"

Zeke glanced overhead and was struck by how a sky so clear could cast a shadow so cold.

"Almighty, He got a grip on this colored man, and He wringin' me like clothes in the lye-soap water. If He can't clean me up, He throw me in the wash-pot fire."

A troubling silence fell, except for a whistling wind and the rattle of saddles as the horses struggled through deep drifts.

"That what this is about?" Will finally asked. "Seein' if there's anything worth savin'?"

From the suggestion of self-loathing in his tone, Zeke figured there was more than one of them who was sure of what Will had conjectured.

"You hurtin' lots of ways, ain't you, Mister Will."

He looked at the Slash Five hand and found Will staring back, the blue eyes like windows into a cold room that had forgotten how to be a home.

"Master said it's always good to tell what's ailin' you," Zeke added.

"You sure hadn't done much tellin'."

Zeke lowered his head, remembering and regretting.

"Looks of things," Will went on, "you got plenty hid in your woodpile if you're callin' this just deserts. Whole world went to hell and gone since you showed up."

Zeke looked up, finding Will framed against a burning sun that gave no warmth.

"No, sir, Mister Will. The world went to that awful place soon as Master went slidin' down that post."

"Did what?"

"He was like a pappy to me. Never had one, you know, least none I remember. Mama gone and died when I was nine, then I didn't have nobody. Still workin' the fields, but I played with the horses ever' chance I got. I was still a young'n when Master learned I was a ridin' fool. He say, 'Zeke, you come work the mossy-horns with me.' He picked me out, sure did, but it was same as pickin' a spot out for hisself in the graveyard."

"That what you done here?" pressed Will, his every word an effort. "Picked one out for the both of us? All we need's a little dirt kicked on top."

Zeke began to shiver even worse than the day before. It was one thing to shoulder blame voluntarily, but to hear someone else castigate him was an unbearable load.

Zeke went silent, and he held his silence on into afternoon as the horses carried them through a howling white desert that lay under the sun like a blinding looking glass. With every swirl of powder about his pony's legs, every scrape of stirrup-high drifts against his boots, the reflective surface punished Zeke's face from all angles. By mid-afternoon his eyes began to water, and soon neither blinking nor dabbing could slow the flow. He had lost his ability to see, the world reduced to a blurry dispersion of terrible light.

Unable to navigate, Zeke relied on Will's lead and his own horse's native intelligence. He clung within a length of the bay's hazy form for mile after mile, his eyelids twitching uncontrollably. He felt as if someone had poured a bucket of sand in his pupils, but this was the kind of grit that not even tears could wash away. The pain was excruciating, but that in Will's jaw must have been just as severe, judging by the subdued moans that continued to crawl up from someplace deep inside.

They went on that way, a frozen-jawed cowboy and a blind one, until Zeke didn't think he could endure another moment of the Appaloosa's rocking gait. Then the horse stopped, refusing the squeeze of Zeke's thighs that should have prodded it on, and all the black rider could do was squint into wildly scattered light that told him nothing.

"You there, Mister Will? I be like a just-borned kitten."

Zeke already knew the answer before he asked; Will's moans had guided him all afternoon. Still, Zeke was relieved to hear the cowhand's voice, although he could barely make out the words.

"Made it to the fence. You stomp the wires down for us?"

"I know you' feet's awful, but I can't sees. Sun sure bounce off of that snow."

Will gave a labored sigh. "Two of us together wouldn't make a whole cowhand. Here, I'll lead your horse up there by the bridle."

As soon as Zeke felt his Appaloosa advance a few steps and wheel into a stationary position, Will's tortured voice sounded again.

"Boss Man must be out for blood. Your eyelids is all swelled up like a horse kicked you."

"Last time I could sees, he'd got you right flush in the jaw. He a mean one, that critter is."

"Fence post beside you if you can get down."

Stiff from cold, his own feet like frozen ham hocks, Zeke nevertheless managed to dismount. He groped for the fence, hanging his glove in a barb, and then worked his hand along the wire to the post. The bottom strand was flush with the snow and his feet were without sensation, but he planted his boot close to the staple and stamped the wire free. He did the same for the next strand, but the uppermost ones demanded a gloved grip on either side of the post before he wrenched out the staples.

By touch, the wires had a definite sag now, but not enough to take a horse across. Feeling his way on down the fence, Zeke freed the strands from a second post before he was satisfied with the slack.

"I holds it down with a foot if you can step 'em across," he said.

Zeke was only vaguely aware when two large shapes crossed in front of him, but soon he dragged himself back in the saddle for the final leg of their ordeal.

Between snow blindness, frostbitten feet, and a future that didn't seem worth living, Zeke wondered if it would have been better never to have returned from the Big Drift. But as the

Appaloosa splashed across the Middle Concho and Zeke caught a whiff of mesquite smoke, his spirits rose.

"They smoke comin' out of the shack chimney, Mister Will?"

"Damn, never would've believed it." Will's voice had new-found energy. "Figured we's the only ones made it in."

"Any horses you know?"

"Couple back side of the trap lookin' peak-ed. Guess we'll find out soon enough."

The smell of smoke grew stronger, a salve to Zeke's spirits, and soon he heard the rattle of tin that told him they had reached the shed and horse trap.

"I helps you off and unsaddle, if you be my eyes," he said.

It was the only partnership possible in order to do the right thing by the horses that had seen them through. Nevertheless, challenging minutes passed before Zeke escorted the half-dead animals into the trap. Facing the drifting smoke, he accepted Will's arm about his shoulders—just as Zeke in turn placed a supporting arm around the Slash Five cowhand's back—and the two men helped each other toward the line shack.

The rock steps were still glazed, no easy thing to negotiate for a cripple and a half-cripple, but as soon as Zeke heard the door screech open he used the last of his reserve to help Will inside.

"By god, y'all been through it, ain't you?"

Zeke didn't think he knew the voice, but he had no trouble recognizing succoring arms that relieved him of his burden and supported his weight.

"Obliged to you," he told the person assisting him.

Helped across the room, Zeke contacted a cot frame, and for the first time in what seemed forever he sat down in a hospitable environment. Still, it did nothing to restore his vision or ease his misery. If anything, it accentuated his travails, for now the instinctive drive to survive, which had masked much of the pain, began to subside.

"What outfit's this, anyhow?" asked a second voice. "The two of us been trailin' our stuff all the way down from the Sweetwater. You two seen any Half Moon cows?"

Zeke flinched as if he'd caught a two-by-four between the eyes. What little warmth that had soaked through to his blood fled like a runaway bronc. He wanted to shrink to the size of a bug and crawl away, because that's exactly what he was—a bug about to be squashed. But there wasn't a blessed thing he could do about it except sit condemned and blind and wait for it to happen.

The Half Moons on Sweetwater Creek had belonged to Master Young.

They had caught up with Zeke. They had tracked him across the months and all those miles, and now he would feel the burn of a hangman's knot. His feet would dance in the air while women gasped and schoolchildren stared in wide-eyed fascination. The men he had ridden with would gawk alongside, pondering how this colored man could have betrayed such a nurturing person as Young.

Betrayed.

Would Vennie be there too, dwelling on his betrayal of her trust? At the spring of the trap door, would her satisfaction be greater than anyone else's? Would any of Zeke's concerns even matter anymore, considering that he would be getting exactly what he deserved?

As Zeke sat cowering, stricken by a blindness that denied him the dignity of even reading the realization in the faces of the Half Moon riders, a strange thing happened.

Nothing.

Zeke listened, studying the cowhands' voices as

they talked with Will. One man echoed Master Young's South Carolina accent, although this Carolinian was clearly uneducated. The second stranger had an odd way of sucking on his teeth. That, and his difficulty in pronouncing *th,* suggested that a bronc may have kicked out a tooth or two.

Zeke had never worked on the Half Moons, but he had crossed paths with a few of its drovers over the years. He combed his memory, vainly trying to identify any of them with the traits displayed by these men. It was true that a hoof could have taken out the second man's teeth only recently, giving him a speech impediment he'd never had before. If that was the case, his lack of reaction could have been because Zeke's swollen eyes had rendered him unrecognizable.

"Half Moon cows." The Carolinian brought the topic back around to the drift cattle. "Seen any this way? We're talkin' a half moon open at the bottom."

The other man sucked on his teeth. "Burned in the left shoulder."

"Can't say as I did," Will struggled to reply. "Zeke?"

Zeke cringed again at the mention of his name. A threatening silence gripped the shack, a deadly hold that seemed to cut off his windpipe. Now they would know. They would put two and two together and come up with a scaffold and dangling rope.

"Zeke," Will asked again, "seen a Half Moon?"

Shaking his head, Zeke turned his face away and passed a hand across his aching eyes. *No, sir, Mister Will, but they's done seen me.*

"Guess our cows is halfway to Mexico by now, Quint," said the man with the speech impediment. "I say the hell with 'em."

"By god, weather don't turn worse, me and Taylor will start back in the mornin'," said the Carolinian, obviously addressing Will. "Your camp's been a lifesaver."

Or a stairway to gallows manned by conniving hangmen, thought Zeke. Were these Half Moon riders just toying with him as a cat did a mouse?

Blind and scared, Zeke shuddered.

Will was in such pain that everything was a fog.

The cot creaked as he tossed and turned, unable to find a position to endure the discomfort. His feet and jaw had warmed, restoring feeling in the form of a constant, dull ache growing worse by the minute. He just didn't know how much of this he could take. The Almighty could have thrown him under a milling herd or cast him to the snow and been done with him, but Will supposed that his penance wouldn't have been complete. As much as Will loathed himself for

110

his role in that Texarkana night, somebody obviously loathed him more.

He was glad the two line riders from up north had taken advantage of age-old custom and made themselves at home, even though the Slash Five crew had been away. Just getting a fire going would have been daunting. As it was, the strangers not only kept the stove stoked, but offered up hot coffee and broth, the only nourishment feasible for a man with teeth that seemed ready to explode.

The Half Moon riders also accomplished something else that Will would have been hard-pressed to do on his own—remove his boots and socks. But one look at his feet was enough to make Will wish they were covered again. The skin was bluish white, especially at the toes, and blisters stretched up to his ankles. Most were filled with milky fluid, but some seemed to hold blood.

Will figured it was just as well that he couldn't see his jaw.

Ever since Zeke had removed his own boots, he had lain facing the wall. One Half Moon hand, evidently experienced in treating snow blindness, prepared a salt poultice for his eyes. But even as Zeke accepted it, he did so without turning. Will guessed that any light, even a kerosene lamp and a fire showing through a stove's cracked cast iron, was too painful to face for somebody in Zeke's condition.

In clear-headed moments that night, Will stared into the dark and saw faces. Major Hyler's was the most vivid, a troubled face that strangely looked a lot like Will's own. Maybe it was the defeat in the eyes, the kind that builds when a man searches for redemption he can never have. But Arch's features were powerful as well, and even those of surly Wampus.

Could they have survived? If he and Zeke had made it back, even at terrible cost, might one or two of the others still do so too?

At daybreak, after stoking the heater and ensuring that Will and Zeke were fixed on wood, water, and eats, the Half Moon hands set out for their home range. No sooner had the rattle of their saddles died away than Zeke stirred in his cot and rolled over, showing his swollen eyes for the first time since the evening before.

"You awake, Mister Will?"

"Closer to dead." Just forming the words stressed Will's aching jaw.

"Sorry I brung this on. Boss Man blinded me like He done preacher-man Paul. I be like the house built on sand that He a-blowin' down, and I drags you right in the middle."

Even across the room, Will was sickened by the appearance of Zeke's feet. For good reason, he resisted the urge to look at his own.

"He's takin' His pound of flesh, all right. Can't see nothin' at all?"

"Can't bear to open my eyes, the light hurts so awful. But I sees a lot on the insides. I sees how mad the Almighty is with me."

Will considered his own issues right now—his jaw and feet, his concern for the missing cowhands, the smell of kerosene that he could never wash from his hands.

"Figure you're not the only one He's riled up at."

As Zeke fell silent for a few seconds, Will, too, looked inside himself and didn't like what he saw.

"Mister Will, you ever wish for a do-again? A chance to do somethin' different if you could?"

That long-ago fire seemed to blaze once more.

"Ever' damned day."

"I goes back just a few months, do just one thing over again, my Vennie's probably wakin' up beside me right now."

Will heard again all those pitiful screams as the fire devoured.

"Least you're wakin' up, alone or not. Some not ever wakin' up."

Will closed his eyes, dwelling on all the events in his life that had led to this moment. A do-again. He knew right where he'd start, but couldn't imagine how different the years might have played out.

He looked again at the Negro who had such a way of making him search inside himself.

"You've rode a lot of trails," said Will. "Say you could go back, take the right fork instead of the left. Expect it'd make any difference, time we rode this far? If we was the same SOBs turned the wrong way before, who's to say we wouldn't've took a even worse trail the next fork?"

"You forget. We can still go traipsin' off the wrong way. And makin' that awful turn once upon a time might be the sure 'nough reason we have to keep on turnin' left instead of right."

Will lay pondering Zeke's words for troubling seconds. "So we just playin' out our hands, that what we're doin'? 'Cause we went this a-way instead of that, can't do nothin' except ride right straight on to hell?"

"Maybe so we's already there, Mister Will."

Will shuddered. He had shuddered a lot since he had looked up from that barbed wire and seen the black rider. If this was hell, then Zeke had been sent straight from those Texarkana flames to torment him.

"What is it you got against me?" he probed.

"I don't know what you mean."

Will wished he could look into Zeke's eyes. A man could tell a lot about a person by what his eyes showed when challenged by an uncomfortable question.

"You said you dragged me in to this," Will went on. "You keep sayin' you're sorry. Quit tellin' me you don't know what I mean."

"I ain't got nothin' against you, Mister Will. It just be the Almighty. He after me awful bad. A big cyclone start a-turnin', it sweep up ever'thing in its path."

Will sat up, the pain in his jaw throbbing worse. "You got somethin' to say, say it! Straight out, damn it!"

"You got hants, just like this colored person do. I ain't no more ready to pull 'em up out of the grave than you is."

For all of the Negro's tendency to talk in riddles, at times he spoke with a lot of truth. And Will knew that this was one of them.

As the day dragged on, the ache in Will's feet intensified to the point that he would have given a year's pay for someone to bring him a bucket of snow. He seemed to recall hearing that rubbing a frostbitten area with snow was good for healing. As things were, all he could do was toss and moan and accept his punishment.

When he needed to heed nature's call, he found that his feet just wouldn't support him. Fortunately, an empty coffee can served the purpose of a slop bucket, which Arch had said educated folks called a chamber pot.

If it hadn't been for Zeke, Will guessed that he would have refrozen today, and done so without food or drink. The Negro seemed to have a way of keeping him just enough alive to hold up under the carefully measured torture Will meted out from his own memory. Although Zeke's twitching eyelids were still swollen shut, he managed to feel his way around on obviously painful feet long enough to stoke the fire and bring Will the warm soup of watered-down beans.

Another miserable night passed, finally giving way to a morning that greeted Will with a throbbing in both feet. He had been determined to ride out in search of the others today; an able and responsible cowhand would have done nothing less. But damn it, he still couldn't stand, so how the hell could he expect to help somebody even if he found them?

Throughout the morning, Will's guilt grew as he lay helpless. If a man rode for a brand, he looked out for his own, whether it be cattle, horses, or fellow cowhands. Especially cowhands. It didn't matter if they were good men like Arch and the Major, or sorry ones like Wampus. They were his partners in a hard life, and if one of them was in trouble, he was supposed to do something.

But it was left to a virtual stranger—from a race that Will had been raised to believe was shiftless and irresponsible—to take the first step.

"I might be able to get on my horse today," Zeke said. "Uneasy 'bout the others."

Will stared at him with newfound admiration. It was true that the swelling in Zeke's eyelids had gone down, but his eyes were still pinched.

Not only that, but he stumbled around like a blind man on tender feet that couldn't have looked worse if they had gone through a sausage grinder.

With all the nagging pain in Will's jaw, it was still a struggle to talk, but there was only one thing he needed to say.

"If you can boost me up on my horse, I might can go with you."

Zeke turned, looking so pitiful with those eyes squeezed shut. "I don't want to argue with you, Mister Will, but you can't even stand up."

"I can still set a saddle. And I can see, which is more than I can say for you."

"I can holler, though. You ain't even got a voice. You better stay put—don't want to lose them feet."

Will felt a rush of blood to his face and he sat up. "Only a damned coward would lay here while a blind man does what he ought to be doin'."

"Way you chased after Mister Major, nobody could ever say you a coward."

"I'm worse than one. You don't treat a mad dog the way I done that night." The admission slipped out so suddenly that Will didn't even realize what he had said until Zeke responded.

"What night's that, Mister Will?"

Will was glad that Zeke couldn't see his face; it would have spoken the cold, hard truth about Texarkana no matter how Will tried to shade his words. Even so, he decided his best response was none at all.

"I had to shoot me a hy-phoby dog once," said Zeke. "Poor thing a-sufferin' like he was, best thing for him."

"I never was taught mercy," Will said quietly. "Least, not any that made sense to me."

For a moment, Will was back in those dogwood shrubs, shoveling dirt over burlap bags of bones at the bottom of a hole.

"Best thing for them," his drunken father was saying between swigs from a jug. "I let them loose, wouldn't've been able to fend for theirselves. The Yankee sons a bitches! Damn them to hell for makin' me do this!"

"My master." Zeke's voice broke through Will's nightmare. "He say teachin' don't have nothin' to do with it, that kindness is somethin' you either got or you don't. Even then, you liable to do wrong sometimes."

Will pondered the words as the scent of that fresh-turned dirt lingered in his memory. "So if a man done somethin' so bad once that he don't even deserve to live, he still might have some good left in him? How would he know?"

"Master say the Almighty puts a whisper inside us. We do somethin' shouldn't oughta have, the little voice say so. Guilt tell us we still got a soul left."

Will lowered his head and wondered. If guilt

118

was any measure of the goodness he still had hidden away, he had more of it than any preacher man. As much as he wanted to believe it, though, he knew better. He had far too much punishment due him, and it was time to offer himself up for more.

"I get my boots on, we'll rope us out some horses. Make a lot of miles before—"

The door popped open so suddenly that Will almost shed his skin. He looked up quickly, wondering why the Half Moon riders had come back, and was stunned to see Arch stumble in, followed by Wampus. They were walking corpses, with frost clinging to faces marked at cheekbone and nose by blue-white flesh.

"What the hell!" exclaimed Will.

"Winter burns a deep brand," muttered Arch. "Flesh and all."

"Just the two of you?" Will asked in haste.

"Not that many if you tally the parts that aren't frozen."

"Major—you seen Major?"

Only now did Will notice the rapid twitching of Arch's eyelids.

"I can't even see you, Will."

Just a piece here, a piece there.

That was all Zeke seemed to have left, just scattered shards of himself. The big freeze had claimed its share of his body, and events had taken an even greater measure of his life, leaving nothing but fragments, tatters, disconnected parts.

He just didn't think he could ever put any of them together again, not while his insides stayed in such turmoil.

When Arch and Wampus had burst in, Zeke had died a dozen deaths. Better had it been the Half Moon riders delivering judgment than the Slash Five hands bearing a story of a chance rendezvous at an abandoned line shack without firewood. At least with a rope around his neck, Zeke wouldn't have to live every moment in dread.

The moment he wished such a thing, though, tremendous guilt struck him. Was this what he was now, a shell of the person Vennie had known? One looking to grab any chance of mental well-being, even if it cost two more men their lives?

Vennie! Vennie! What done gone and happen to this colored person?

She wasn't there to tell him, but Zeke knew the answer anyway. All the guilt reminded him that he still had a soul, but it was a dark soul already given over to the devil.

The weather had been just as cruel to the returning cowhands as it had to Zeke and Will. Arch suffered from not only snow blindness, but frostbitten fingers and toes. Wampus's ears were a fright, according to Will, but his feet also told of too many days in the kind of cold no man was meant to experience.

The next several days were miserable for all of them. For the most part, they lay around, trying to outlast the effects of their ordeal. Little by little, Zeke's eyes improved, although he remained sensitive to bright light. But there was no escaping the pain of his throbbing feet except in sleep, and that came only in fitful spurts. Throughout, the cold kept its terrible grip, even without additional snowfall, but finally seasonal temperatures returned.

"Major's not comin' back, is he."

Day had broken warm in the line shack, and the four men were sipping coffee black enough to float a horseshoe. Zeke, too, had dwelled a lot on the Major's fate, but it had been Will who had finally stated what Zeke figured everybody already knew.

"Major never was coming back, Will," said Arch.

"Sure lost a good man, Mister Major was," said Zeke.

"Lost more than that," observed Will. "The Slash Fives don't have a manager no more."

"I've been contemplating that," said Arch. "It's imperative we notify the owners in New York."

"I know. Arch, you're better with words than we are. You up to ridin' thirty-five mile into San

Angelo and sendin' a wire? Way you're feelin', maybe you won't get sidetracked by the girls like we did last time. Early spring, we got a cow hunt in store, likes of which we never seen. Owners got to know."

The general roundup had been on Zeke's mind as well. For months he had fled, trying to put as many miles as possible between him and Master Young's slumped body. For a while, the brush with the Half Moon riders had given him reason to continue his flight. But with every new day, his expectations of their return had diminished, until he finally realized that it just wasn't going to happen. Now, another good man had joined Master Young in glory land, and in one of his last acts the good Major had hired Zeke for a job—chasing after the Slash Five herd.

Maybe Zeke had every right to consider his obligation over now, freeing his conscience to leave. But he didn't see it that way. There would be a roundup on the Devils in a couple of months, and Zeke knew he needed to be a part of it. He had already let down Master Young, and he didn't intend to make the same mistake twice.

Weeks passed as the Slash Five range seethed with bloated carcasses that festered in the heat of day and refroze at night. The late December snow had seemed to promise good seasoning in the soil for spring grass, but it had been a dry snow with little lasting effect. Meanwhile, the skies went barren, except for distant clouds that built day after day low in the south, and even the springs on the Middle Concho became trickles.

The wind began to blow, a suffocating gale choked by the stench of death. It kicked up swirls of dust that rose higher and higher, until the winter sun threw only a strange twilight across country fit only for a boneyard.

There was just gloom and death, like a jumping-off place to hell.

It was a fitting place to work for a man already damned, Zeke figured, and even without cattle, there was plenty of work to do. Harvesting cowhides was the most pressing chore, for soon warmer weather would come, hastening decomposition and inviting maggots. Even as things were, it was a race to save as many as possible from a sky thick with vultures. In minutes, their sharp talons and powerful beaks could rip and shred beyond what the hide agents in San Angelo would accept.

All a good skinner needed was a horse, a couple of lengths of rope, and a sharp knife, along with a neckerchief tied across his nose to make the stench a little more bearable. Zeke had all the essentials this morning as he reined up before a stretch of drift fence where cattle had bunched and died. There must have been ten or twelve in the pile, a rotting mix of cows and steers. Only a couple were Slash Five beeves; the other brands were unfamiliar and spoke of origins on faraway ranges to the north. Still, as he considered the work to be done, he didn't discriminate between carcasses. Ownership in drift country ended when an animal died, and when spring came, northern outfits would have their hands full hunting beeves on the hoof rather than worrying about hides.

Zeke began by tying onto a bloated cow's stiff hind leg and dragging the carcass away through shadow tracks of circling buzzards. The dust billowed up, thick and bitter. It stung his eyes and singed his nostrils, but the stirred odors were no less unkind, hanging in his throat on their way to the pit of his stomach. If ever there was a sign that the whole world was ruined, this was it, but

Zeke didn't need any help recognizing that fact. He could feel it deep down in his dark soul.

When he had the dead animal positioned near a sturdy post, he dismounted and loosed the rope. Setting to work with his pocketknife, he skinned the feet first, and then did the same to the head, undressing the hide down to the neck and around the shoulders. After splitting the belly, he secured the horns to the post with a short rope and tied his lariat around the hide bunched at the neck.

Mounting up, he used the horse's power to bring the lariat taut and peel the hide back farther. After accomplishing a foot or so, he stepped down and trimmed it with his knife. It was a nasty job that required repetition and careful attention, but the hardest labor consisted of climbing on and off his horse so many times.

Finishing, he draped the hide over the fence and stood admiring it for a moment, taking pride that he had already offset his day's pay by the dollar or so it would fetch. By the time the sun set in a fiery haze, he could earn his keep for a whole month or two.

Zeke heard a quick whish and something settled around his shoulders and drew tight. He felt the burn of rope fibers across his chest an instant before a powerful force yanked him backward. His cry died in his throat as hide and fence surged upward. The next thing he knew, he was flat on his back, the suffocating dust flying as jarring ground raked across his back at frightful speed. Sky and sun tossed wildly to the drum of hoofs. He couldn't breathe. His very bones shook like a rabbit in the jaws of a dog determined to kill.

Zeke was cowboy enough to realize what was happening, but he didn't understand why. But the reason didn't matter, not when any second his skull would find an unyielding rock or uproot a stump. Dragged at rope's end by a galloping horse may not have been the best way to die, but it was one of the surest. For a split second he was conscious of the hazy sun burning in his eyes, and then the sky went black and he wasn't aware of anything anymore.

When Zeke came to, he was trussed like a hog, his hands secured at his back and tied to his uplifted feet. He felt so helpless, squinting up at the swimming sun and spitting out dirt, but when he felt a noose drawing snug against his windpipe, he knew this wasn't over yet.

"You got somethin' I want, nigger boy."

The words came from behind, and Zeke tried to squirm around to see as the voice persisted.

"All that time, I thought they was somethin' about you I should've knowed. I'd ever studied that face of yours good, I'd've figured it out quicker."

Zeke visually followed the catch-rope at his neck up to a saddle horn and the dally hold of a cross-eyed rider with a dribble of tobacco juice against his sloping jaw. He was no more than thirty, but he had the swollen nose and splotchy face of a man who had spent years looking in a bottle. But it wasn't until he spat tobacco juice through broken front teeth that Zeke understood the reason he slurred every *th* sound.

"Rode all the way back through the snow thinkin' on it," the man went on. "Up there for weeks goin' about my business, that black face of yours poppin' into my head." He sucked on his teeth. "Then somebody on the Half Moons says, 'Wonder where Nigger Zeke run off to with the old man's money?' They'd heard all about it, but wasn't a one of 'em knowed what he looked like. I kept my mouth shut, but right there's when I put two and two together and knowed where I'd seen you before. Bet you wish I'd never drove that Half Moon bunch to the Red, turned 'em over to you and Young that time."

Zeke didn't have any memory of him on the Red River; he knew him only as the Half Moon hand who had identified himself as Taylor at the line shack. But that didn't change a thing.

"You takin' me back to Mister Hang-'em Man?" Zeke asked.

The rope dug into Zeke's throat enough to make him gurgle. "I'll damned sure do it right here and now if you don't talk."

Zeke could feel his eyes bulging as he thrashed to the upward pull of the rope. *Vennie! Vennie!*

127

Taylor relaxed his dally hold and eased the pressure at Zeke's neck.

"I . . ." Zeke wheezed, momentarily unable to find air enough for words. "I don't know what to tell you."

Zeke felt another jerk of the rope.

"The money, you clabber-head! What did you do with it?"

"Ain't got it no more. I swears."

"Likes of you couldn't've ever spent it. First time you flashed it, been a dead giveaway you took it off some white man. You want me to hang you? That what you want?"

Taylor trembled in rage, and Zeke stared into those uncoordinated eyes that flashed one way and then another, and told him the truth.

"That gold cursed. Just like I is."

"I'll show you cursed!"

This time the power of the horse was behind the rope, and the world began to go dark as Zeke felt the rasp of the moving turf.

"You ready to talk?"

The words seemed to come up through a great funnel, but when they reached Zeke's ears he was ready to bare everything. Still, between his empty lungs and the smothering dust, he couldn't respond until Taylor had hurled more threats.

"I . . . I puts it in a dead cow."

Taylor glanced over his shoulder. "You take me for a fool? They's ever' which way! Where is it?"

"Up the line yonder. Maybe mile."

Taylor stepped off his horse and approached with his pocketknife. Zeke shrank, expected Taylor to slash his throat, but the man only severed the tie between his hands and feet. Zeke's wrists were still bound at his back, but at least he could move his legs again.

Taylor dragged him up roughly. "Start walkin'!"

Zeke shuffled through the dirt just ahead of the horse, the catch-rope still connecting his neck to the rider's dally hand. His feet throbbed with every step as Zeke dwelled on matters.

It was only right about that money. The only chance he stood of squaring things with the Almighty was to see it returned to Master Young's widow. Even if it was too late to make amends in this life or the next, it was still the right thing to do, maybe the last right thing Zeke could ever do. His only regret was that he was being forced into it, rather than doing it of his own free will. That kindly woman who had been Master Young's wife deserved his best, and Zeke had let her down.

Finding one carcass among hundreds wasn't easy, but at least he was searching for something dead a year or two instead of weeks. Just when he thought that rotting cow must have gotten up and ambled away, he pulled up before it. He studied every detail—the big spread of horns as dusty as they were mossy, the hollowed-out eyes and bared teeth, the dried piece of tongue that buzzards had yet to find. But most of all Zeke saw the exposed ribs with just enough parchment to hide what was inside.

"Maybe so this gold make Master Young's wife feel some better," he said.

"Wife, hell," said Taylor, dismounting. "Who put that notion in your head?"

Zeke turned and stared into those crooked eyes, windows into a crooked soul.

"You ain't takin' it back, is you." The realization came suddenly, shockingly. He glanced at the snaking rope extending from his neck. "You ain't leavin' nobody to tells on you neither."

"Out of my way!"

Zeke stepped aside, helped by a rough hand, but he did so with a word of caution.

"Sure like holin' up in them places in wintertime, them rattle-tails do."

Taylor had already knelt to insert a hand, but he didn't stay long.

"God A'mighty!" he exclaimed, recoiling and jumping up. "The hell I'm puttin' my hand in there!" He clutched Zeke's shoulder and spun him around. "You'll dig that stuff out or by god I'll drag you to kingdom come!"

Zeke felt a tugging at his wrists. His bonds were stubborn and Taylor's fingers overly anxious, but with vicious cursing the man finally freed him. Zeke was still roped by the neck to the horse, but at least he could rub his raw skin now and try to restore circulation. Taylor cut his efforts short with another oath and slung him toward the carcass.

Zeke dropped to both knees before it, visualizing what was inside and dwelling on the evil man hovering over him. Zeke himself had denied Mrs. Young the future that Master Young would have given her, and now this son of hell would take from her even the small comfort the money might offer.

Zeke was at the end of the line, the end of a rope destined to kill, and there was only one right thing to do.

He plunged his arm to the shoulder inside the carcass and withdrew it just as quickly. For a split second he faced Taylor, a crooked eyed devil-of-a-man framed against a gloomy sky swirling with sand. Then Zeke's ears were ringing, deafened by sudden thunder that rocked him to the core.

Zeke could already smell the gunpowder as Taylor doubled over and the knees gave way. He could see the powder burns at the belly of the man's shirt, but Taylor hadn't even hit the ground when the rope snapped tight at Zeke's throat, jerking him across the crumpling body. The Schofield revolver in Zeke's hand had delivered justice, all right, but at the price of a spooked bronc bolting with somebody else who had a debt to pay.

Bouncing and twirling, Zeke knew he would be choked into unconsciousness in seconds if he didn't do something. He threw a hand up along the rope, trying to ease the tension, but sky and ground continued to whirl through the raging dust. On the dodge all these months, he had expected a hangman's noose sooner or later, but he had never dreamed it would be this way.

Zeke still clutched the six-shooter that had killed Master Young, and with every twist of his body it gouged and pummeled. He managed to cock it and squeeze off a wild shot, and when the bronc shied and cut sharply, its hind legs tangled in the rope.

Now the threshing hoofs were in Zeke's face, ready to cave it in, but it was a toss-up as to whether he would know it when it happened. He was lightheaded, everything fading, the rope at his neck wrenching the life from him. He thought he heard a revolver roar at point-blank range, and then he was back in Vennie's arms, reliving one last time the happiest moments he had ever known.

When Zeke's wits returned, he found the bronc's motionless silhouette blocking the sun. Its hind leg was only inches away, streaming with blood from a wound on its hock. His shot must have made the bay pull up lame, but that didn't mean the horse didn't have the strength to bolt again.

Zeke wanted to calm the animal with soft words, but with a rope at his larynx he could manage only a disturbing guttural. Avoiding sudden movements that might alarm the horse, he worked frantically to spread the loop, but tense moments passed before he succeeded in slipping it over his head.

Zeke stood, finally able to speak reassuring words, and worked his way along the animal's side to the dragging reins. He checked the rear leg again, finding the wound only a nick, and then looked back over his shoulder. Before the fence a hundred yards away, Taylor lay under the ominous sun, from all appearances one more carcass among hundreds waiting for the maggots and buzzards.

Zeke mounted up and rode back. He didn't want to go near the body, didn't want to see what he had done, but he had no choice.

Dismounting, reins still in hand, he crept up from behind as if that would negate his part in this. Taylor lay face down, a blood pool soaking the dirt where it had oozed out beneath him. Except for the ruffle of his stringy hair in the wind, he was perfectly still, but the stirred ground all about told that his final moments hadn't been easy.

Zeke would rather have faced that awful blizzard again than touch him, but he forced himself to roll the body over. The crooked eyes were open, staring at him. But they were also dilated, and when Zeke laid a hand on the chest and found no rise or fall, he breathed his own sigh of relief that he didn't have to kill him a second time.

Zeke stood and studied his surroundings. A few yards down the fence line, five or six long-horn carcasses lay scattered. The buzzards had already feasted, rendering them worthless to any hide hunter who might come along. Tying onto the man's legs just above the worn boots, Zeke climbed into the saddle and dragged the body closer. By rope and horse, he set about rearranging the dead cows, burying Taylor as effectively as shoveling dirt into a three-by-six hole. There would be a smell, all right, growing worse with every warming day, but in a slaughterhouse such as this no one would ever notice.

Zeke had raised so much dust in his efforts that the blood trail and spot where Taylor had bled out were already covered. If only the accumulating dark stains on Zeke's soul could be blotted out as easily. . . .

He had one more thing to do before he put this dreadful site behind him. He slipped the revolver back in its hiding place, and then rode away with a vow to figure out some way to return the money belt to its rightful owner.

In minutes he was back at his skinning location with a tender-legged horse he wouldn't be able to explain. After retrieving his hat and own mount, which had wandered, he unsaddled Taylor's animal but kept the bridle in place. Leading the Half Moon bronc through a nearby break in the barbed wire, he freed the gelding. A hard slap on the rump sent the animal on its way, and a few well-aimed rocks kept it going.

The saddle, Zeke disposed of just as he had Taylor, interring it under vulture-rent carcasses. One killing had led to another, and as he positioned the final bloated cow across the cantle, he couldn't help wondering if there would be more men he would have to bury the same way.

"What in hell you doin', Zeke?"

The voice was stern, challenging, and Zeke started and whirled. He had made such a commotion dragging the carcasses into place that he hadn't heard Will ride up. But there he was, straddling a stocking-footed roan, his eyes piercing as the dust swept between the men.

"Zeke," Will demanded again, "You better tell me."

Zeke stepped off his horse. There were times when a man just couldn't lie, but that didn't mean he had to tell the full truth.

"Mister Will," he acknowledged.

Zeke traced his catch-rope to the dead cow's leg and began to loosen it. "I drags the buzzard-eats off of the good ones and piles 'em on old saddle here."

He heard the stocking-footed roan come closer.

"The look I got, I'd swear it's more than that," accused Will. "Body or somethin'."

Again Zeke spun, this time convicted by what he had done just a mile or so up the fence line. Guiltily, he looked down, hoping his eyes hadn't betrayed.

"No, sir, Mister Will, just a old saddle, sure is."

"Where'd it come from?"

Zeke stood, avoiding eye contact as he coiled his lariat.

"I just rode up on it." Praying that would be the end of it, he tied the coil to a saddle string.

"Wasn't Major's, was it?" The skepticism in Will's voice may have faded, but not the energy. If anything, there was even more, and when

Zeke turned in growing fear, he found the Slash Five hand swinging off the roan.

"Drag that last cow off of there," said Will. "I want to get a look at it."

"Just a beat-up saddle, all she is, Mister Will."

Zeke faced Will, who proceeded to look him up and down.

"You're all skinned up," Will observed. "Shirt's tore up too."

Zeke felt a web of lies beginning to settle over him.

"Bronc here swallowed his head, sure done it. I reached for the horn and catches myself in the seat of the britches when I hits the ground. Arm tangled up in catch-rope, sure 'nough, and off he go to the races."

Zeke didn't know how convincing he was, but Will had another matter to press.

"Let me see your rope. I get it tied on, drag that cow on off."

Zeke was shaken by where this might be headed. Sure, there was nothing but leather under there, but for the life of him, he couldn't recall whether it had the sheen of a kack fresh out of a saddle shop, or the cracks and weathering that would support his story. Not only that, but there was a horse blanket with it. Could the wool still show the bronc's foamy sweat? And what about the serviceable bridle and lariat that were sure to raise questions?

There was only one thing Zeke was certain of as he swung into the saddle. Intentionally or not, Will was forcing his hand, and to do so to a desperate man could have consequences too terrible to think about.

He glanced back, watching the Slash Five hand kneel and secure the loop around a stiff hind leg. A vivid image suddenly burst into his mind's eye, and Zeke was stricken with fear.

Vennie! Vennie! I don't want to bury no more men!

He stood in the stirrups and dug his knife out of his britches. It flashed in the muted sunlight as he unfolded it, and in another moment he had the blade against rope, ready to slash it and spur his horse away from awful temptation.

"Can't stop thinkin' about Major," spoke up Will, tightening the loop. "Can't stop thinkin' how I let him down."

His words were enough to make Zeke hesitate and then surreptitiously withdraw the knife.

"I . . . I knows what you mean," he whispered, remembering not just one good man, but two.

Will stood and turned with all kinds of regret in his features. "We should've done somethin', Zeke. I ought to done somethin'. I sat right there on my horse and watched him ride away to his grave."

"No, sir, Mister Will. We both set a-watchin'."

Will's hat brim began to fall, hiding his

troubled face. "Why the hell's it so hard to do the right thing sometimes?"

The right thing. If Zeke started figuring up all the right things he hadn't done, he didn't know how high he would have to count.

"It's bad enough what you get drug into when you're not even growed up," Will continued. "Get to be a man, decide for yourself, still don't know what's right or not sometimes."

"Think He a-keepin' count, Mister Will?"

"Who?"

"Almighty. He got a tally book, you think, keepin' track of the bad we done? You . . . You reckon He write down the good too and tallies 'em one again' the other?"

Will shook his head. "Make no difference how much is on the good side if there's a awful enough thing to blot it all out."

If that was the case, thought Zeke, by now the Good Lord had already stopped bothering keeping track on the pages with his own name at top. Zeke might keep trying to bury all the bad in a bunch of dead cows, but he knew he hadn't hidden a thing from the One who would decide his just rewards.

In surrender, he squeezed the horse with his thighs, and the slack rope rose from the ground and tightened. The bronc went only a few paces, but the carcass followed amid billowing dust. In moments it was there for God and man both to see—a scuffed saddle with a pronounced swell that gave a rider an advantage in clinging to an unruly animal. Then Will was squatting before it, tracing fingers along a weathered cantle that collected the settling grit.

"Climb in and shut the door," he muttered.

Turning, Zeke stared, his confusion as great as his nervous anticipation.

"First form-fitter I've seen in a while," Will continued as he rose. "Nothin' Major ever rode. Get down in one of them, shut the door like they say, it'd take a sky-jumpin' bronc to unseat you."

He glanced up at Zeke, and then looked back at the saddle. "What I hate's not just the not-knowin'," Will added. "There's all that other stuff in my head—what I didn't do and ought to have, and what I shouldn't done but went ahead anyhow."

"Guess we's all got a lot of hants, Mister Will."

"Yeah, and I guess they'll chase us all the way to kingdom-come before it's over."

Or to hell-come, thought Zeke.

12

The burdens on Will were so heavy that he didn't know if he could last another day.

First, there was the physical travail of every waking moment. His teeth and jaw had improved, but the steady throbbing in his feet wouldn't let him forget what Arch had said: "Frostbite in December, amputate in June." To hear Arch tell it, it took that long for dying tissue to separate from the living. Will just hoped he got away with losing no more than a toe or two. It would have been a hell of a thing for a cowboy to try to climb in the saddle with nothing to go in the stirrup.

Then there was the guilt that followed Will even into his dreams. He continued to relive his dark boyhood each time he looked at Zeke, but he also kept finding Major everywhere—in distant yucca, in every night noise outside the line shack, even in old saddles rotting underneath carcasses. Just last night, Major's eyes had peered at him out of a wall of flame in his nightmares.

Will had a pretty good idea why Major was increasingly on his mind. The New York owners had wired orders that he assume Major's duties as boss of the Slash Five wagon in the general roundup, and on this mid-February day, he was sitting in the cattlemen's association's annual planning meeting in San Angelo.

Will didn't know how the responsibility had fallen on his shoulders, and if he hadn't owed Major an unpayable debt, he never would have agreed. But here he was, a working cowboy in linsey-woolsey shirt and duck trousers, completely out of his element among all the haberdashery-fresh owners and managers in a smoke-filled hotel chamber. The way their mustaches were trimmed, the barber must have done a booming business. Will, isolated on the Slash Fives all winter, had never been so self-conscious about his ragged hair, and he wished he would have at least sharpened his razor a little before shaving.

Debt or not, he would have sooner forked a green-broke bronc on a frosty morning than squirm in so hard a chair and pretend he belonged.

Still, when J. H. Rayburn edged into the aisle, Will leaned forward, ready to hang on every word. A lanky man in his mid-forties as bald as an eagle except for a ring of graying red hair, Rayburn had earned his respect through the cow-savvy he had shown in last year's roundup. As Will had heard it, Rayburn had cut his teeth on drives up the Pecos, a dangerous enough journey without the Comanche bullet he had ridden into at Horsehead Crossing in the sixties. He still had a decided hitch in his gait as he made his way up front.

"Gentlemen," he began, picking at his mustache, "this won't be no regular cow hunt. Cattle drifted, they drifted bad, and the drift fences couldn't stop 'em. They come down from the Sweetwater and the Pease, the Canadian and the Cimarron, and some even say the Arkansas. From Colorado on down through the Panhandle, the country don't have a cow left in it, I expect.

"Now, a lot of these beeves bunched up on the Pecos, but just about as many struck the head draws of the Devils and trailed 'em out all the way to the river. That's where all our stuff went to, the Devils, but they's so mixed in with drift cattle from up north that we's lookin' at the nightmare of all nightmares."

A hefty, bespectacled man who looked as if he had never sat a horse rose from the front row and adjusted his stylish vest.

"May I jump in here a minute, Mr. Rayburn?" he asked, turning to the attendees. "I'm the cattlemen's association secretary, if there's any newcomers here, and I just want to say that ranch managers as far away as Nebraska have been writing and asking the roundup plans. So just remember that whatever you decide here needs to accommodate untold scores of partnering outfits. I venture to say the scale of the roundup will be just as unprecedented in the cattle industry as the drift itself."

"You're plum' right about that," said Rayburn as the secretary sat again. "I was down on the Devils early this month, and you ain't never seen the likes of it. Cows was strung out thick as heel flies the whole twenty-odd mile between Beaver Lake and them old fort walls, Hudson they call it. I'd bet a month's wages you could tally up a couple of hundred thousand easy."

Rayburn made a few jaws drop, and Will's was one of them.

"They was still showin' fair flesh but they'd done eat near' all the winter grass, so they's gonna be sufferin'," Rayburn continued. "But we can't just worry about forage on the Devils— they's eighty mile of dry plain we got to push 'em across just to bring 'em back up as far as the feeder draws for Dove and Spring creeks. Sure save a lot more head if we was to hold off till late March, give spring rains the chance to green things up some, fill up the water holes."

Will cleared his throat and wished Arch was here to speak for him.

"I hear the Half Circle 6 on Dove Creek's startin' for the Devils next week," he allowed. "All the Spring Creek outfits too."

Every head had turned to Will, so he was glad when Rayburn responded and deflected attention.

"Got ever' right to go after their own cows," said Rayburn. "But my feelin's that it's gonna be like pickin' needles out of a haystack, they's so many foreign cattle. I think we got to push 'em all out of that river valley first—*canyon's* more like it—and not even try to sort any till we get back in God's country, Dove and Spring creeks. They don't call it the Devils down there for nothin'."

The secretary rose again. "May I make a suggestion? I'm an attorney, not a cowman, so I don't profess to understand all the practicalities of a roundup. But a late March date as Mr. Rayburn outlined would give me a chance to contact the interested ranches up north and allow them the time to get work crews here.

"And keep in mind, gentlemen, it's unlikely that any of them have been to the Devils River before. It might be prudent to meet at a place easily found and march on to the Devils together."

It all made sense to Will, and after listening to more discussion, he joined in electing Rayburn general superintendent. At daybreak March twenty-eighth, all participating outfits were to strike out from the VP, a Spring Creek ranch eleven miles southeast of the Slash Fives. From there, it would be a hard journey south-southwest to roundup headquarters at Beaver Lake, the Devils' northernmost watering point.

145

Will sure hoped the spring rains Rayburn talked about came, because otherwise the eighty-mile return drive would be a death march for thirsty cattle.

After the meeting, Will caught up with Rayburn in the hotel lobby.

"Don't suppose in your rounds to the Devils and back you come across any sign of Major Hyler?"

The flaring ends of Rayburn's red mustache dropped, and so did every crease in his ruddy face.

"Sure did hate to hear about Major. Now there's a man deserved ever' bit of the respect people give him. I'll tell you what I did see—they was a roan, saddled and bridled, dead down there on the river. Buzzards had got to it, though, so I couldn't make out the brand."

Even in the trail's-end cowtowns on the Kansas railroad, Zeke had never seen so many cowhands. But he had never known such dust either.

It had marched with them for days now, all the way from pecan-shaded Spring Creek, and with every strike of hoof against tableland, another plume rose to catch in Zeke's throat and further distort the blazing sun of late March. Although distant clouds had continued to build south of the Slash Fives into early spring, the expected showers had failed to bless other areas. Zeke was here by choice, of course, but he felt sorry for all the horses trudging without complaint under the weight of at least three hundred riders bound for the general roundup.

Zeke also pitied the plodding teams that pulled the chuck wagons, loaded with not only bedrolls but enough supplies for weeks on the Devils. Then there was the remuda, over a thousand strong, stirring its own dust a half-mile ahead and off to the side. Unburdened, these spare animals had it the easiest, but before long the individual outfits would rope out fresh horses and mules for their turns under saddle or harness.

The grit filled Zeke's eyes and worked its way down inside his sweaty collar, bitter alkali that already chafed. And for mile after mile, it turned the cracked beds of dry water holes into dance halls for dust devils.

An outfit was known by its cattle brand, which was usually distinct from that of its horses. As a result, Zeke wasn't sure which ranches were represented on this march. But he had heard enough talk to know the rivers these men had started from: the three Conchos and the Colorado, the upper Brazos and the Pease, the Canadian high in the Panhandle and the Cimarron above the state line. But it was the Arkansas in the reaches of Kansas that struck him most, for he had heard Arch say that an Arkansas River cow would have had to march six hundred miles to get to the lower Devils.

Six hundred miles.

Zeke didn't doubt it, because he had driven South Texas cattle to Kansas enough times. But what he couldn't grasp was that cattle had done it on their own, defying drift fence and unknown country with no guide but instinct and a blizzard at their rumps.

So far, even in the evenings, Zeke had sequestered himself alongside the Slash Five bunch—Will, Arch, Wampus, and a few other men. Despite his determination to fulfill his obligation to Hyler, he had done a lot of soul-searching to find the courage to saddle up that last morning at line camp. He kept reminding himself of Taylor's claim that no one else on the Half Moons could identify him as Master Young's colored person. But Zeke wasn't so sure, and all he could do was keep his hat brim low and shiver at the thought of all the cowhands around him who might ride for the Half Moons.

He wondered if a person thought about something hard enough—feared it enough—he might actually make it happen instead of ward it off. He didn't know if a man had that kind of power, but that was before a horse came loping across from the line of chuck wagons and a quirt-lean rider with scraggly goatee came abreast.

"By god, thought that was you two, by god," mumbled the cowhand through a tobacco-swollen jaw.

Zeke didn't recognize the pronounced cheek-bones and hollowed eyes, but the backwoods voice crossed with a South Carolina accent was unmistakable. A chilling dread swept over him, but all he could do was look away and keep his chin down behind his shielding brim.

"Quint, isn't it?" acknowledged Will. "Figured the Half Moons would be sendin' a wagon."

"How's them god-awful feet? See your boot's

still wrapped around somethin' at least, by god."

"For now, anyway. Might not have turned out that good, wasn't for you and your partner seein' after us at the line shack. He come down with y'all?"

Zeke heard Quint give a half-laugh.

"Funny thing, damned funny thing about that Taylor. He kept scratchin' at his head all the way back from your camp. I'd say, 'Taylor, what's eatin' at you? You got the lice?' And he'd say, naw, he was just tryin' to figure somethin' out. Got back to the Half Moons—half-froze ourselves—he kept actin' funny thataway. Then one night he ups and disappears. Didn't draw his pay or nothin', by god. Just throwed that ol' formfitter of his across a Half Moon horse—stole him, you might say—and lit out. Least, they was both gone in the mornin', by god."

Zeke suddenly had a hard time breathing. His heart seemed ready to explode through his chest, and he had to restrain a powerful instinct to touch spurs to horsehide.

He heard Will's words even before the Slash Five boss voiced them.

"You say form-fitter? Come across one on the Slash Fives several weeks back. Layin' up against the drift fence down there just below us. Don't guess he had any reason to come back through our country?"

"Hell, who knows. Taylor was about as loony

as he was mean. And he was mean as a one-eyed snake sometimes."

Quint rode away, but Zeke wouldn't look in his direction until he was sure that the distance and dust obscured.

Wampus snorted from the withers of an Appaloosa. "We hang a damned horse thief these parts."

"The language of deterrence," spoke up Arch, bouncing with the gait of a gray gelding. "We've been known to hang to stirrups and even hang a quarter of beef, but vigilante justice rings of dime novels rather than fair knights of the range."

"Hell," snapped Wampus. "What I'd give to hear you speak English for once."

At midday the procession dropped into a rugged drainage that slowed the chuck wagons. Still, they rumbled on, and in midafternoon Zeke and his companions intersected a half-mile-wide valley startling in its contrasts and contradictions.

The slopes of the bordering hills rose gray and barren, a desert burned by the searing sun, while in the valley bottom a three-hundred-yard grove of live oaks thrived green and massive along with willows and mesquites. The mott fronted a small lake, a couple of acres glinting in the sunlight. But there was something strange about this pool, shimmering in the glare like a living thing in constant motion. All the bellowing should have been a clue, but not until Zeke rode closer did he realize that the shallow lake stirred with cattle wedged shoulder to shoulder from one side to the other.

"Lawdy, Lawdy, I ain't never seen the likes," he said.

"If a man was to tell me this, I'd call him a liar," added Will.

"All I can distinguish is head, horns, and a ribbon of backbone," assessed Arch. "The heel flies, I presume, have most definitely revealed the soothing protection of H-two-O."

"Damned things has chased 'em to the water too," offered Wampus.

But even as Zeke remained astounded by life numbering in the thousands, he was equally struck by how this valley of the Devils was a place of such death. Winged shadows crisscrossed his path, cast by a sky swarming with buzzards. Their brothers feasted on cattle carcasses so numerous that a man could have jumped from one festering mass to another as far as Zeke could see.

He had no choice but to fall into line behind Will in single-file march that chased vulture after vulture into flight. Zeke had yet to rid his hands of the smell of all the cows he had skinned, but this was the kind of stench that burned his sinuses and churned his stomach.

The scene was grim enough, all right. But

before they drove the surviving cattle eighty miles back across scorched desert, untold thousands more would mark the way with their bleaching bones.

"I reckon this is Beaver Lake?" Zeke pondered aloud.

"Got to be," said Will. "Riverbed just widens out here, looks like. Don't run a lick above here. Below it either, till you get several miles down-canyon, they tell me. If you listen good between the cows' bawlin', you can hear the springs feedin' the lake out of the hills."

"So's how come they call this the Devils River?" asked Zeke.

"Not so long ago," spoke up Arch, "it was the River Saint Peter."

"The fellow a-standin' at them glory land gates?" Wampus asked incredulously.

With so much death pressing in on all sides, Zeke felt more as if he had just breached the walls of hell, and he must have said as much out loud.

"Amen, Brother Zeke," said Arch. "That echoes the sentiments of the first Texans through here in the forties. 'Saint Peter, hell!' one of them remarked. 'Looks more like the devil's to me!' "

Zeke trembled, because he knew that Lucifer may have just summoned to his dark bosom the already damned.

In minutes they reached the gnarled live oaks that once may have been an Eden but now seemed like paradise lost. Surveying all the dead cattle, Zeke figured a Chicago slaughterhouse couldn't have been more revolting.

"Don't expect me to lay my bedroll out in this do you?" griped Wampus.

Zeke had been thinking the same thing, but he wasn't about to voice it. Will, for his part, chose to ignore the complaint, instead turning in the saddle and looking back up-canyon.

"Wagons is havin' a time of it, so much dead stuff in the way," he said. "A couple of you men ride back and give them a hand."

Zeke started to rein his mount, only to see the four trailing hands already starting toward a scene all too familiar—carcasses plowing the dust at the end of lariats drawn taut by horse power.

"I'd refrain from disappointment, Zeke," said Arch. "Our opportunity awaits. Here comes Superintendent Rayburn with urgency in his demeanor."

Sure enough, a big black horse with a mustached rider was loping up and powdering the turf.

"Will," said Rayburn as he pulled rein, "you're bossin' this outfit, ain't you?"

"So they tell me," said Will.

Rayburn's mustache twitched as he scanned the area. "All these dead cows got to be drug out of the trees," he instructed with a sweep of his arm. "We'll pile 'em up in the open and set fire to 'em. Don't see how them nesters up yonder stand it."

When Rayburn pointed back through the mott, Zeke made out an old shack framed against the north ridge.

"Anyhow," the superintendent went on, "we got to have us some decent camp grounds. We's gonna be workin' this river awhile."

"Yes, sir," said Will, squinting as he studied the crowded lake through overhanging limbs. "A right smart while, looks like."

"One other thing, Will. First light tomorrow, I'm ridin' downriver, checkin' things out far as that ol' fort. Be takin' a few men with me."

Will made eye contact again. "If you're askin', I'll be ready. Like to see that dead horse if you can find it."

"Thought you would. Let's hope I can."

14

Every step of the way, the valley of the Devils looked like the aftermath of a terrible war.

Will, riding in a party of five, supposed it *had* been a battle in a way, a fight to the death for the canyon's limited grass. Still ongoing, it was a conflict with no victors—neither the bloated carcasses that the daybreak buzzards were already fattening on, nor the living skeletons of the West's finest herds waiting their turn for talon and beak.

Around the first major bend, the dry gravel of the riverbed yielded to a pool of putrid water floating with dead cattle. It was the first in a series of carrion-ridden water holes scattered over the next couple of miles. Will could only imagine how the pools normally sparkled in this fringe of the Chihuahuan Desert, where water usually meant life instead of death.

All the way from Beaver Lake, the riders traced an old mail road that repeatedly crossed the intermittent stream that did a snake-track dance through a place of few trees and many cacti. Will wondered if the frequent side canyons offered better grass, but full daylight revealed rocky gulches with more dead cows than live ones. Still, more cattle than he could count roamed the country in desperate search for forage.

As the morning wore on and the strewn limestone of the lechuguilla hills radiated a sun worthy of a wasteland, the riders began to string out to accommodate the paces of their respective mounts. Just as the canyon turned southwest, Quint from the Half Moons dropped back to join Will on drag.

"Say, how long you had your colored boy?" Quint asked.

"Showed up the day the big freeze come on," said Will.

"Just a few months then. Know anything about him? Where he come from?"

"Don't even know his last name. All I ask of a man's a hard day's work, and he gives me that and more."

Will's last statement had a touch of regret in it. The truth was, ever since he had inherited the responsibility of wagon boss, he had looked for a reason to figure up Zeke's time. But Will was honest enough with himself to know he couldn't send even this grim reminder of a dark past on his way without cause. There was more than Zeke's admirable work ethic to consider; over the winter, the strange bond he had forged with

Zeke during the blizzard had grown stronger, no matter how much Will had fought it.

"By god, I didn't want to say nothin' in front of him yesterday," said Quint, "but I think Taylor has his suspicions about him."

"What do you mean?"

Quint took his hat off and brushed his sleeve across his brow.

"Taylor gets a chance, he can drink more whiskey than Sweetwater Creek runs water. His tongue will loosen up and he'll spout off some big bear story he won't remember nothin' about next mornin'.

"By god, he got to tellin' me one night over a bottle how a colored boy shot and killed the Half Moon owner in the Red River country—man by the name of Young. Supposed to made off with a poke full of gold from the sale of a herd."

Stunned by where this was leading, Will reined up and faced the Half Moon hand who stopped with him.

"You sayin' it was my man?" he pressed.

"Taylor sure thought so. Claimed to have met Young and his colored boy once. Said his name was Zeke Somethin'-or-other, and that your hand was a dead ringer for him."

Quint shook his head and then continued. "By god, Taylor wanted me to go in with him and catch that boy of yours by hisself and make him cough that gold up. I was three sheets to the wind and he about had me convinced. Then I woke up with a straighter head and realized half the colored boys in Texas is named Zeke and Taylor can't tell 'em apart any better than I can. I never said nothin' more about it, by god, and Taylor didn't neither."

Quint continued to talk, but Will was too busy trying to digest what he had already heard to listen any more. He began replaying all of Zeke's words and actions to see if there could possibly be a connection. He had seen nothing about the Negro to suggest he was capable of killing somebody for his money, but he knew firsthand that a dark corner could lurk in any man's heart.

That Zeke carried some troubling secret, there was no doubt. He had said so himself, in so many words. But a mistake that cost a man his job or a friend or a chance with the right girl was a far cry from turning a gun on a person. Anyway, if Zeke had made off with a boot-load of gold, what was he doing working from you-can-till-you-can't for six bits a day?

Will supposed he could ride into San Angelo when they got back and talk things over with the sheriff, but that was weeks away. In the meantime, all he could do was keep an eye on the Negro and see if he did anything to warrant suspicion. The way things looked on this river right now, Rayburn couldn't have too many roundup men, and Will had to concede that Zeke was nothing short of a top hand.

Soon the canyon veered west, and then north of west, before curving south again between four-hundred-foot bluffs and narrowing to perhaps a third of a mile. Near its westernmost bulge, perhaps fifteen miles from Beaver Lake, Will and his companions rode upon a magnificent pecan grove at the lower end of a lagoon. The pool, situated at the base of an imposing hill that defined the canyon, would have been beautiful if not for all the dead cattle around it. Through the tall rushes at water's edge, Will could see the kind of color that one didn't often find in a drouth—green lily pads floating on a bright blue surface that meant a constant inflow of fresh water.

Oddly, the lagoon was a couple of hundred yards off the Devils channel, but it nevertheless formed a river of its own that surged along the bluff until Will lost sight of it in the pecans. Somewhere down-canyon, he figured, it had to join the Devils proper.

"What they call the Pecan Springs," said Rayburn as they held their horses. "Here on down to the Rio Grande, seventy, seventy-five miles I expect, Devils don't ever quit runnin'."

But a living river didn't mean grass, at least not very far off its banks, and even if this valley had once been the equal of a tall-grass prairie, the invading army of cattle would have long since shorn it to nubs.

Trees, however, could tap underground water, and the results downstream of the springs were astonishing. Will and his party rode on, periodically passing through towering timber that would have been the envy of even the Texarkana woods. This far south, the deciduous trees were already fully leafed, representing not just pecans, but huge cottonwoods, elms, sycamores, ashes, willows, and mesquite. Will was most impressed by all the live oaks with massive trunks that three men joined fingertip to fingertip couldn't have reached around.

But as refreshing as the shade was for mile after mile, the constant lowing of starving cattle was as discouraging as the silent testimony of those already dead.

In early afternoon the riders splashed their horses across a beautiful, tree-shaded ford, which Rayburn called Second Crossing, and ascended a fifty-foot bluff up out of the wooded bottomland. Here, where a west-side canyon yawned, a complex of crumbling walls marked a sprawling flat overgrown with scrub mesquite. The difference in temperature was striking, for the guarding hills left and right were like hot rocks throwing heat back on a fire. Why the US Army would have built a fort in this natural oven would have been a mystery to Will if he hadn't noticed all the driftwood in limbs forty feet high from Pecan Springs on.

Forage was as scarce here as anywhere else, but buzzards and rotting beeves were not. The dead stretched from ruin to ruin and on inside the canyon to a distant rock corral. There didn't seem to be a blade of grass to be found, but that didn't keep hundreds of scrawny longhorns from looking. Everywhere there wasn't a dead cow, there was a live one with its head to the ground and its tongue wrapped around the barest hint of a nub.

It was a sad sight, the dead and the dying awaiting scavengers under ghostly walls that would be their only gravestones.

Rayburn led the riders up to the old pens and halted. The stones still stood chest-high in places, but elsewhere time had breached the walls. As soon as Will pulled rein, he could feel the radiating heat of the sun-baked blocks that helped ripen nearby carcasses that were in varying stages of vulture-shredded flesh. Only one set of putrefying remains seemed out of place among the rest.

"Will," said Rayburn, nodding to it, "I think this is what you come for."

Will dismounted with a troubled reverence and tied his mount to a scrub mesquite. The rotting head and barrel-like rib cage were of a horse—a roan like Major's, from what little hide was left.

Not only that, but it was still saddled and bridled, as if its rider hadn't lived to tend to the animal.

Will didn't have to kneel and inspect the cracked leather, but he did so anyway. He had admired Major's hand-tooled saddle from the start, and back in the fall he had put a little money aside in his war bag for a down payment on one just like it at the San Angelo saddle shop where Major had purchased his. Will's big ideas, along with his savings, hadn't lasted past the spree on his next trip into town, but his admiration for Major's saddle had never waned.

Will ran his fingers along the cantle, feeling the weathering and remembering. Zeke had been right to rope Major off his horse. Had Will had that kind of courage—the kind to do whatever he had to—Major never would have disappeared into those snows. Maybe all of them would have died trying to save him, but that would have been better than adding one more wrenching regret to all those that he had borne since he had been ten years old.

Shaken more than he had expected, Will stood and scanned the scorched flat with its silent ruins.

"Wish all these walls could tell me somethin'," he said quietly.

"Like whether that horse is Hyler's?" asked Rayburn.

Will continued to study the post grounds and its festering dead.

"It's his, all right. What I want to know is if he climbed off of that thing when it died."

"His, is it? Damn." Rayburn found a deep breath. "Like as not, he fell off and died back on the divide. I'd say his horse come all this way by himself and starved to death from that bit in his mouth."

Still, Will studied the immediate area. "You look around any when you was here?"

"If you mean for a man, just about five minutes is all."

Now Will turned and faced Rayburn and the others. He hadn't even been aware that all of them had dismounted, but there they were, holding their horses and looking tired, sweaty, and flushed by the searing heat.

"I know we're goin' to be pushin' dark-thirty as is, gettin' back," said Will. "But I'd like to give this fort a goin' over. If y'all don't feel like you can, that's all right. I just know I can't ride off without doin' it."

Each of them was a cowboy, with a cowboy's sense of responsibility, so Will was not surprised to see everyone mount up and fan out in search. Will paid the series of ruins special attention, because he knew there was something about a building—even a roofless one—that drew a man in trouble. He found lots of crumbling, lime-mix bricks and melted adobe, along with a couple of rattlers and more dead cows, but nothing to suggest that a man had stepped inside since the last soldier had marched away.

A full hour passed until the riders gathered where the old post road lay poised to drop off the plateau to the bottomland greenery. Will was the last to arrive, and he rode up still glancing back over his shoulder.

"Done all you can do, I expect," said Rayburn.

It was nice of the superintendent to say so, but Will knew differently. He could have done more, a lot more that day in the snows.

"Let's get the hell out of here," said Will.

Without waiting for a response, he bent his shoulders and urged his horse down toward Second Crossing and faraway Beaver Lake.

15

Zeke had never dreamed of rounding up cattle this way.

He had his horse belly-deep in Beaver Lake, and the animal pushed through the water at such an angle that it forced succeeding bunches of beeves toward shore. The other Slash Five hands were there too, encouraging the cattle with whistles and sometimes none-too-gentle words.

At first the respite from the heat had been a welcome change, but as the novelty began to wear off, Zeke considered other aspects. He had crossed a lot of rivers on the trail to Kansas, and they had all been fraught with the unknown. Current dynamics and tricky underfooting could challenge the best rider. Even though Beaver Lake was placid and had a gravel bottom, there was always the possibility of an unexpected hole that might upend his mount the next step.

In the meantime, Zeke's misery tally rose by the second. He had already spent so much time in the lake this afternoon that he didn't know if his worn boots would ever dry out, or how cracked the leather would be if they did. He could only imagine how prune-wrinkled his feet would be when they finally saw air again.

But Superintendent Rayburn had dished out powders to round up the first trail herd from the lake, and Zeke couldn't disagree. With hundreds of heel-fly-inflicted cattle constantly ambling in and out, cowhands didn't have to bother flushing them out of the brush and feeling the slap of thorns. Even more important, the beeves were rested, watered, and already at the departure point for the parched divide and faraway Dove and Spring creeks.

"Will, patience may be a virtue, but mine is about depleted."

Arch straddled an Appaloosa several yards to Zeke's right, where the water was deepest. The four of them abreast—Arch, Zeke, Will, and Wampus in the shallows—rode at a forty-five-degree angle to shoreline. They were like a long spoke of a great wheel, with Arch on the faster-moving outer edge and Wampus nearest the hub. So far, the method had proven effective in sweeping scores of beeves to solid ground where other riders could take control. Arch's position as point man was most dramatic, splitting hundreds of deviled-horned beeves either left toward shore or right toward the lake's center.

When Arch got no response, he said it again.

"My patience, I say, is about—"

"Give out already?" asked Will. "You're havin' all the fun out there."

"Oh, the bath is pleasant enough, notwithstanding that Saturday hasn't arrived yet—or has it? But I'm speaking of your reticence so far in telling about that horse you went to locate."

"What horse is that?" asked Wampus.

Zeke didn't know either, so he was glad somebody asked.

"Nothin' to tell," said Will, whose suddenly subdued tone was clearly not of a man who wanted to discuss it.

"Was Rayburn able to direct you to it?" pressed Arch.

"What horse?" Wampus asked again.

"Yeah, he was," whispered Will, still shunning eye contact.

"Dead with a saddle and bridle still in place?" asked Arch.

Zeke had listened with mild curiosity up to this point, but as the implications struck him he whirled to Will.

"Mister Major's? You done gone and found his horse, Mister Will?"

Will rode in silence for long moments, his head and shoulders sagging. Then he reined up, forcing everybody else to pull rein to hold formation. He glanced at Wampus on his left before facing Zeke and Arch with a lot of scoring at his misty eyes.

"We done a terrible thing, men," he managed. "A god-awful terrible thing."

Zeke first looked beyond Will at Wampus, and then around at Arch. It was the latter who asked the question that suddenly burned in Zeke's mind.

"Are you referencing yesterday? Or the winter past?"

Will lowered his eyes. "When . . ." He shook his head, as if trying to drive the emotion from his voice. "When you ride with a man, he's supposed to be able to depend on you. When he's in trouble, he's supposed to be able to depend on you."

"You tellin' us it was Mister Major's horse, ain't you," said Zeke.

"Will," Arch asked compassionately, "did you find him, bury . . ."

Will shook his head again. "But he's still just as dead."

Now he did turn his distressed eyes in Zeke's direction, but the Negro couldn't tell if he looked at him or Arch or both.

"We just let him die," Will continued. "Damn us to hell, we just let him die."

Zeke had come to feel that way as well, and his hand on the saddle horn abruptly went out of focus. The list of men who would have been alive if not for him was growing longer all the time.

"Will," said Arch, "you mustn't allow yourself to harbor such guilt. When there arise circumstances beyond one's control—"

"That's just it, Arch," interrupted Will. "We could've done more. We should've done more."

Will turned his face to the sky, a thin ribbon glistening on his cheek. Suddenly emotion began to collect in Zeke's throat.

"You right, Mister Will. We could've hogtied him across his pony and dragged him back. Done had the catch-rope on him, we did."

Will faced him again, but the words barely would come.

"I . . . I did somethin' else wrong that day, Zeke. I treated you like a, I don't know, a dog, I guess. You roped him off of his horse and was willin' to do what it took, and I wasn't."

"Quit it, Will," chastised Arch. "You want to know the consequences had we continued in ill-advised pursuit?" He waved his arm toward the far shore, where buzzards tore at hide and flesh. "That would precisely have been our fate."

Abruptly Will's eyes were hard on Zeke, and they stayed fixed even as he responded to the other cowhand.

"Maybe . . . Maybe that's all some of us deserve, Arch."

Lord A'mighty, that sure 'nough's the truth, thought Zeke.

"We're losin' our cows, boys," Will said quietly.

Zeke started his horse forward with the others, but he hadn't managed a half-dozen paces when Arch's Appaloosa squealed. Zeke found the bronc thrashing wildly, rearing and lunging in water that tossed like a flood-swollen river. Arch was already crooked in the saddle as he fought to bring the terrified bronc's head up.

"Hold him, Mister Arch!" exclaimed Zeke, turning his horse toward him.

"What in hell!" somebody yelled.

"Cottonmouth bit him!" cried Arch. "He—"

But now the horse was down, and so was Arch, hidden in water that continued its wicked swirl. Abruptly something emerged from the whirlpool, a snake slithering on the surface and leaving a wake as it bore toward Zeke. He met it with the double of a rope, but the triangular head with its piercing, dark-lined eyes was almost in his lap before he caught it flush.

Zeke didn't know where the pit-viper went, or if the next thing he would feel would be its fangs in his leg. His focus now was on the Appaloosa that he saw only in flashes in frothy water that had swallowed it. The lake was only withers deep, but the horse couldn't get its head above water, regain its feet—and Zeke suspected the reason why.

Arch was down there, pinned to the saddle, and if something didn't change quickly, he would die a terrible death. Already a flailing hoof may have caught his skull.

Finding his pocketknife and opening it, Zeke dived at the next flash of the Appaloosa's head.

He caught the animal around the neck and held on for the wildest ride of his life. He didn't know that a living thing could wield such power and fury. It was as if the horse was bent on drowning the three of them. For a while there was nothing but bubble-filled water everywhere, and then Zeke glimpsed daylight, felt a rush of air, heard a squeal quickly muffled by more water. Seconds later Zeke found the Appaloosa's throat and drew the knife across it, a slash as quick as it was deep.

For what seemed forever, the horse thrashed even more violently, but all Zeke could do was cling there holding his breath and tasting blood mixed with water. Finally the animal's death throes relaxed, and Zeke came up for a quick breath and a glance around. There was no sign of Arch except for his floating hat, and Zeke dived again, knowing Arch would be in even worse straits if the dying bronc pinioned him against the lake bed.

Through murky water darkened by the horse's brute shape, Zeke skimmed along bottom. Sure enough, the animal sank as it ceased its struggles, and when the lifeless head settled against the bed, Zeke pulled himself across it and groped for the cowhand. Fortunately, the Appaloosa hadn't pinned Arch, but Zeke found a body alarmingly languid with a foot caught in the stirrup.

Zeke didn't take time to try to work it free. He severed the stirrup leather with his knife and surfaced with Arch limp in his arms.

Will was there, standing almost neck-deep in glinting water that swirled red.

"Lord A'mighty!" Will exclaimed, reaching for them. "Arch! Arch!"

They rolled Arch to his back and supported him under the shoulders as they pulled him toward shore. When his boot heels dragged dry gravel they stretched him out on his back amid a gathering crowd.

"Drowned. Damn sure drowned."

The voice and shadow belonged to Wampus, but Zeke had too much to do to look up. He dropped to his knees with Will and found color in Arch's features, but also an ugly mark at his temple where the bronc must have kicked.

"Arch!" cried Will, patting the unresponsive face. "Arch!"

Zeke brushed Will aside without apology. "I gotta get here!"

Zeke laid his cheek close to Arch's mouth and nose and placed a palm on the cowhand's chest. He knew that time was critical, but he forced himself to wait and listen and feel.

"Don't find no breathin'!"

Zeke scooted around until his knees were in the gravel a foot or so beyond the crown of Arch's head. Lifting the victim's arms, he drew them

173

toward him with a sweeping motion that ended with Arch's elbows on the ground at Zeke's knees. The action induced Arch's lungs to expand, but Zeke wasn't through. Rocking forward, he reversed the process, concluding by pressing Arch's bent arms into the chest.

Zeke continued to lift, draw, return, depress, even as he remembered the cold body he had once helped pull out of the Cimarron. The trail boss had performed this very procedure, and Zeke could only pray that this time it wouldn't end with a similar pile of lonely rocks.

"What the hell's he doin'?" grumbled Wampus. "Might as well get him in the ground."

But Zeke was determined. Eventually he would have to give up, all right, but not while he still had the strength to rotate Arch's arms.

He heard approaching hoofbeats that ended with a crunch of nearby gravel, followed by the jingle of spurs.

"By god, what's all this? He get himself drowned or somethin'?"

Not even Quint's voice could make Zeke stop and turn away.

"What's this mumbo-jumbo he's doin' on him?" Quint went on.

"Let him alone! He knows what he's doin'!" defended Will from Zeke's shoulder. "Arch was tellin' me how some doctor come up with this!"

"Too late for playin' doctor, anyhow," groused Wampus. "Better get us some shovels and—"

Arch suddenly jerked spasmodically and drew a quick, groaning breath.

"Lord A'mighty!" exclaimed Will.

With his own cry of exaltation, Zeke turned the wheezing cowhand's head to the side and watched him vomit out water and bile and less pleasant things.

"Easy, Arch! Easy!" said Will with a comforting hand to Arch's shoulder. "You're all right!"

The vomiting spell ended, but Arch was no more conscious than before, and all Zeke could do was remove Arch's bandana and wipe away the dribbling bile.

"Arch! You hear me?" asked Will. "Arch! Arch!"

"Breathin' good," said Zeke, "but he plum' out of it."

Still, Will persisted in saying his name until it was clear that Arch was more than just dazed.

"You suppose bein' underwater like that done somethin' to him?" Will asked.

"He got a awful place where that horse kicked him, Mister Will. Look—that blood comin' out?"

Indeed, blood trickled out of Arch's ear, something that Zeke had never seen before.

"That don't look good," rasped Will, looking up with hopelessness in his ashen face. "I . . . I don't know what to do for him."

Zeke heard yelling, and he looked between

175

Wampus and Quint to see a big roan loping up with an animated Rayburn astride.

"Sandstorm comin', men!" cried the superintendent, slowing just long enough to make eye contact before veering to take his message elsewhere.

Zeke checked conditions for himself. Up past Wampus's sweat-stained hat and on beyond the nose of Quint's sorrel, he saw reddish-brown swirls darkening the sky over the nearby north ridge. It looked to be a booger, the way it was eating away at the hazy blue before his very eyes, and he abruptly remembered getting caught in one such storm that had choked and blinded for twelve hours.

When Zeke turned back, he found Will transfixed by that oncoming cyclone.

"What about Mister Arch?" Zeke pressed.

Still, Will stared. "Lord A'mighty, he don't need to be in this."

"Take him in under the wagon?"

"Worst place for him, way the dirt will be whippin' along the ground." Will's hat brim dropped a little, his eyes refocusing on the distance. "Any you talked with those nesters yonder?"

Zeke craned to see through the legs of the sorrel. Just left of a wooded canyon a couple of hundred yards away, the sagging shack stood against the ridge that had shrunk to insignificance under the rising cloud. Even with three hundred cowhands in camp nearby, the homestead seemed mighty lonesome, and Zeke could only imagine the isolation the nesters faced under normal conditions.

"I reckon we been too busy to go callin', Mister Will."

"That thing's almost on top of us. Let's get him up there."

With Zeke and Will supporting Arch under the shoulders, and Wampus and another Slash Five hand under the thighs, the race was on. Zeke, backing into a building wind, looked down along Arch's torso and up through the frame formed by Wampus and the second cowhand. Quint was there, standing against the shining lake, and his attention was locked on Zeke like a panther stalking an unaware deer.

Quint immediately averted his eyes—more evidence, if Zeke needed any, that his concerns about the Half Moon hand were warranted. Zeke didn't know what to do about it, but with an injured man in his arms and a storm bearing down, all he could do was take it as a terrible warning.

16

The plank floor moved beneath Jessie Alba's bare feet at the same moment that the surrounding walls began to shake.

She stood grinding mesquite beans in a metate her father had found along the Devils, but as the vicious wind barreled through the open windows, she dropped the stone mano and hurried for the shutters. Already, tin plates and thirty-thirty shells were flying from the shelves and the air was growing bitter with dust.

She closed the nearer shutter first, and then sought out the farther across the fourteen-by-sixteen room. Her father Caleb, passed out with a bottle on a rickety bed, never even stirred as she reached across to secure the window.

The door remained open, and normally Jessie could look out and see the sun bright in glassy Beaver Lake. Now, though, there was only swirling dusk. She considered leaving the door ajar, as it was on the lee side, but by its meager light she grabbed the coal oil lamp and matches and closed it. Maybe if she sealed off the draft, the cracks in the box-and-strip walls would draw less dust.

Jessie felt her way back to the table and lit the lamp. By its flickering light, she could see a haze that grew thicker as the sand seeped through with the whistling wind. Already, she could feel the grit between her toes as it crawled up through the cracks in the floor.

The one-room cabin wasn't much of a home, but it was as good as any Jessie had known in her twenty years. Her earliest memories were of an East Texas farm where she had looked into a spring pool and seen features that had set her apart. She had been too young to identify her distinguishing characteristics, but as she had grown older and had spent time staring into a looking glass, she had noted her flat nose and the curls in her dark hair, along with her swollen lips and the small ears pressed against her head.

Jessie looked nothing like her father, except for her natural tan, and the old tintype of her mother had shown a young woman of fair skin and fairer hair. At least that's the way Jessie remembered it from the years before Caleb had thrown the picture away in a drunken rage.

In his sober moments, he sometimes spoke of her mother's rape by a Negro, and of the ensuing manhunt that had left the offender hanging from a hickory tree. But in a stupor once, Caleb had let it slip that no forcible violation had ever happened. Regardless, several months after the incident, Jessie's mother had died giving birth to her, embittering a man already deeply embittered.

Anyone who knew Jessie to be a mulatto might have recognized it immediately, but most people took her for white, although with distinctive features that had softened as she had matured. Still, only Caleb's perception had ever had the power to shape her life, and he had never looked at her with anything approaching love in his bloodshot eyes. Jessie supposed that she was just too great a reminder of betrayal, and worse, and all too often he had proven it by the force of his hand.

Sometimes Jessie felt cursed, a victim of long-ago circumstances beyond her control. From childhood, her lot in life had been so ingrained that it was a wonder she could question it at all. Still, she knew that hers had been a cruel two decades, even apart from the migrant life to which her father had subjected her. He had dragged her from pillar to post, holding down his latest job only until another spree had gotten him fired.

Since late the previous summer, when a Pecan Springs cow outfit had figured up his time yet again, they had nested in this Beaver Lake shack and scratched out a hardscrabble existence that had depended on the fruits of Caleb's shaky aim. Then the invading cattle had come, driving the game elsewhere and polluting Beaver Lake and its feeder springs. For the last several months she and her father had subsisted on boiled water, poached beef, and meal ground from a cache of last summer's mesquite bean crop.

Even day work could have brought in a little money for flour and coffee from a settlement on the Southern Pacific south of the old fort, but Caleb hadn't even tried to hire on with the newly arrived roundup outfits. Over the years, his only motivation to work had come when he had emptied his last bottle.

"Storm, Papa."

Unshaven for weeks, and without a bath or change of clothes for even longer, Caleb looked a wreck. He was thin, drawn, and flushed, with a bulbous nose and dark rot in his dirty teeth. He stirred, mumbling something incoherent, and then rolled over so that the back of his sweat-soaked shirt was to her.

Only now did Jessie consider all the dust collecting in the mesquite bean meal. Just as she covered the metate with two upside-down tin plates, banging erupted at the door.

A remote house in the wilds of the Devils wasn't a place that drew visitors. In fact, no one had stopped by in all these months, even though the property no doubt belonged to some cattle company. Although an entire town had sprung up nearby virtually overnight, Jessie hadn't so much as exchanged greetings with any of the cowhands.

Still, there was that banging, sounding again, this time accompanied by a muffled voice.

"Somebody at the door, Papa."

When he didn't respond, she turned to the shelf and the rust-caked single action Army revolver catching lamplight. Jessie had learned early what the face of evil looked like, and she would take no chances. Taking up the Colt with its five-and-a-half-inch barrel, she concealed it under her apron and went to the door.

She opened it to a hazy pair of troubled faces, one of them black.

"We got a hurt man, ma'am," said the white man.

Sure enough, they supported the shoulders of a third person whose head fell back ominously, exposing his throat. On down below the big rock that served as a step were the outlines of two other men who held the victim's legs.

There had been nothing in Jessie's upbringing to teach her compassion, but somehow she had developed a soft spot for every stray dog that came around. Maybe it had been because she felt so much like a castoff herself, and her sympathy was compounded every time she saw her father mistreat a dog with a vicious kick or hard-thrown rock. Still, she hesitated and glanced at Caleb, who remained as oblivious as ever.

"Ma'am?" pleaded the white cowhand.

Jessie saw something in the stranger's eyes that she almost didn't recognize—kindness. Then she took a moment to study the injured man's blank face.

"He looks in a bad way," she said.

"Yes, ma'am. We got to get him in out of all of this."

Jessie stepped back and pointed past the lamp. "Over in the corner."

She held the door wide, feeling the wind's tug on it as the four cowboys brought the unconscious man up the step and over the threshold. Securing the door, she followed them past the table and lamp to her neatly made cot.

"If you'll move your blankets," said the cowhand, "we won't get them dirty."

"Just lay him on down."

They did so, and as Jessie got a better look she saw mud caking the victim's face.

"What's ailing him?" she asked.

"Horse kicked him in the head and liked to drowned him."

"Need to get the dirt out of his nose so he can breathe."

She took the forty-five out from behind her apron and laid it on the table. As she worked on the tie strings at her back, she looked up and saw lamplight in the cowhand's eyes as he obviously took note of the weapon.

"I'm sorry we scared you, ma'am," he said, making eye contact.

Jessie acknowledged with a wisp of a smile and bent over the injured man. Grotesque shadows played against a wall still coughing sand as she dabbed the blank face with the apron.

"We're obliged to you for all of this," the cowhand added. "I'm Will Brite, and this is Arch layin' here. We're all with the Slash Fives from up on the Middle Concho."

The cowhand's gentle ways invited a response that Jessie normally would have kept to herself.

"Papa over there stuck me with 'Jessie.' Concho's about the only place the old drunk hadn't been fired from."

The shadows of four hats moved against the wall as the men glanced across the room.

"Nothin' wrong with 'Jessie,' " said Will. "They tell me it was my mother's middle name. She died young."

"So did mine."

For a few seconds, there was only the howl of the wind and rattle of the house.

"I know growin' up without a mama don't make things easy," Will added.

Jessie half-shrugged as she moistened the apron with her saliva and tried to work the blood out of Arch's ear. "Life's what it is."

"Yes, ma'am. Guess we got to play the hand

that's dealt us. Too bad more of us can't draw aces."

"Your friend didn't draw any. Blood's still coming out his ear. Don't see any way to help besides keep him easy."

"You're doin' that, Miss Jessie."

Jessie didn't know the last time someone other than Caleb had called her by name, and the two syllables that sounded so vulgar in his gruff voice seemed to take on an entirely different meaning when spoken with kindness. Turning, she looked into the cowhand's eyes with a sad longing for a kind of life she knew she could never have. She held her stare for an uncomfortable length of time, and as Will stared back, she felt the spark of a strange bond with this man she didn't even know.

"Somethin' the matter?" Will finally asked.

Maybe Jessie should have been embarrassed, but no one who had known such abuse could be faulted for a little social awkwardness.

"What the hell is this?"

Jessie turned at Caleb's slurred words, finding him rising to an elbow.

"Brought in a hurt man, Papa. Awful storm out."

"We're with the Slash Fives," spoke up Will. "Sorry to put y'all out. We—"

"What's that in the corner?" Caleb demanded. He burst to his feet, only to fall back to a sitting

185

position at bed's edge. "By god, you bring a nigger in here and I'll kill him!"

Jessie was embarrassed, ashamed. "He just helped carry him in is all."

Caleb whirled left and right. "Jessie! Find me my gun!"

Fortunately, neither weapon was within Caleb's reach, but the black cowhand was already rushing out into the storm.

"Listen," Will told Caleb. "Our man's hurt, and I'm not just goin' to let him die."

Now that the Negro had left, Caleb seemed to calm down. Without establishing eye contact, he waved off Will's remark and reached for his bottle. Still, that didn't keep the other two cowhands from also hurrying out the door.

Jessie wanted to tell the kindly cowboy she was sorry, but how could a person apologize for somebody else? The only thing she could do was resume her ministrations on the injured man.

Will came closer and spoke quietly. "Think we can just keep him here till the storm blows out?"

Jessie glanced at Caleb, who had lost himself in his bottle again.

"He doesn't like colored people." Her voice dropped to a whisper. "He goes to drinking, he's mean as a peat mule."

"I'm sorry we riled him, Miss Jessie."

There was that name again, so pleasant on the lips of this stranger with caring in his voice.

Again, she searched his eyes for the strange hope they seemed to exude.

"Ma'am?" he asked as her gaze persisted. "All right to leave him? I'll come check on him soon's the storm breaks."

Jessie nodded, and as Will stepped back out into the whirling dust, she turned and watched her father guzzle anger-provoking whiskey. For someone trapped in a world such as hers, there could be no end to the storm. It would just go on and on, punishing and laying waste, all the way to merciful death.

Will thought the sandstorm would blow itself out soon, but it raged as if it would never end. He spent the first couple of hours in the saddle, trying to hold the roundup herd together, but as dark fell and the already limited visibility dropped even more, all he could do was rein his pony into the oak mott and seek a windbreak.

From his elevated position in the saddle, he suffered such a scourging in the thrashing limbs that he had to dismount and tie the animal to the first stout bush he could find. Buffeted as he groped blindly, he bumped into the rough bark of a massive oak and edged around to what he took for the lee side. Hunkering down, he buried his face in the bend of his arm and tried to tough it out.

It wasn't easy, the way the wind refused to

follow any set course. It seemed to come from all directions, a living thing that squealed and flailed and threatened to choke him. Pelted by stinging granules, he could only wince with every gust and wonder if hell could be any worse.

As he suffered, he thought of Jessie, and somehow the whipping wind and the bitter grit between his teeth didn't matter as much anymore. Maybe any lonesome cowboy who hadn't seen a woman in weeks would have been smitten by her charms, but Will felt a connection that confused him. He had always felt awkward around a decent woman, but this had been the first time he hadn't known what to say or how to say it.

"When a man's romances have all been on a commercial basis," Arch had opined once, "finding the 'sweet Mary' of his dreams will reduce him to a trembling puppy."

Trembled, Will had, and whimpered too, all before a five-foot-nothing young woman with a simple cotton dress and the most hypnotic face he had ever seen. He loved the way her curls fell across her tanned cheeks, but he was taken most by her dark eyes. Every time she had cast her gaze at him, he had been unable to turn away. But her eyes had been more than arresting— they had seemed to draw him into a wistful soul.

Even now, tortured by the storm all these hours

and hundreds of yards away, that mystifying stare of Jessie's lingered as powerfully as ever, and Will trembled again like a frightened little puppy. But while he shook, he couldn't wait for the wind to stop and daybreak to arrive so he could check on Arch and see her again.

The thought of Arch all but dead raised pangs of guilt. How could any cowhand worth his salt dream of some girl when one of his own may have been fighting for his life? Already, Arch might be lying there cold and stiff, his dilated pupils staring blankly into all the unknowns that death held.

Still, Jessie's face wouldn't go away, for it seemed to stir in him the kind of hope that every man needed in a world that offered so little.

Will was still spitting dust at daybreak, but at least he no longer rocked to a sandstorm as he mounted the homestead step and knocked. It had been a long time since he had so much as tipped his hat to a lady, but as he waited he removed it and held it with both hands at his belt buckle.

The door creaked open and she was framed there, her eyes as captivating as he remembered.

"Miss Jessie," he said politely.

"Will Brite. I mean Mister—"

"No, ma'am, Will's fine," he interrupted. He peered past her. "My man, how . . ."

Jessie opened the door wider and stepped back, and Will took it as a cue and went in. Given the confrontation with her father the day before, he reflexively checked for him over her shoulder.

"He's out with his gun rustling up a rabbit," said Jessie.

Will wasn't sure but that he preferred the ornery devil roaring drunk in bed to the prospect of him bursting in behind a gun barrel.

"Your friend hadn't woke up," she added. "He

was tossing and moaning in the night. Still bleeding out the ear some."

Will went over. The shadows were heavy, and he didn't see the rumpled blanket on the floor by the cot until he stepped on it. Then Jessie opened the nearer shutter and light flooded Arch's face. He didn't have good color, and the purple bruising beside his eye gave him the look of somebody on the way to the graveyard. But fresh blood had massed in his ear, and dead men didn't bleed.

Will took the cowboy's hand. If Arch would just squeeze his fingers, do something to let a body know that his mind was still working.

"Arch, it's Will. I'm here with you, Arch. You hear me? Can you squeeze my hand a little?"

Will thought that maybe Arch's fingers tightened just a bit, but he wasn't really sure.

"We need to get some water down him," said Jessie. "I tried in the night, but he was strangling on it."

Only now did Will realize the significance of the blanket underfoot. Not only had Jessie given up her bed to a stranger, she had slept on the hard floor right beside so she could tend him through the night.

Struck by her kindness, he turned to her.

"The way you've took care of him and all . . . You're a angel, Miss Jessie."

Color rushed to her face so prominently that

191

even someone as backward with women as Will could notice. Even so, he didn't know what to make of it. After all, people sometimes went red out of anger.

But while her cheeks stayed flushed, she stared with those haunting eyes.

"I never liked my name before," she said.

Will figured he hadn't offended her. "Can't say I ever heard a prettier one. You know, you got, I don't know, I guess the eyes a angel ought to have too."

Immediately he realized he probably had said something a little too forward, and he turned and scanned the room.

"Got some water, you say?" he asked.

She didn't respond for the longest, and Will supposed that she still studied him. He would have looked back at her, but he figured one more glance into those eyes would only confound him more. He was glad to spot a bucket in the corner to the left of the door.

"That it over yonder with the cover on it?"

"Already been boiled," said Jessie. "Cup there on the table."

Will dipped a cupful and returned to Arch's bedside without looking at Jessie. He lifted Arch's head and poured a little on the cracked lips, but most of it dribbled down his chin.

"Water, Arch," said Will. "It's water."

Then Jessie parted Arch's lips with gentle

fingers and the next trickle found the injured man's tongue. Arch strangled a little, but he managed to swallow enough for Will to fetch more.

"You and him known each other long?" asked Jessie as they again aided Arch.

"Year maybe. Usually work out of different camps, though." Arch gurgled, and Will withdrew the cup a moment. "Easy, Arch. You don't need drownin' again."

"You really care for him, don't you," said Jessie.

"Can't say me and him even know each other all that well, but no way I'm lettin' him down. You know how it is."

"Can't even imagine," she whispered.

Now Will did look at her, and he didn't hesitate to hold his stare.

"You're awful kind, Miss Jessie. Don't seem like life's done you right. What between losin' your mama, and your father bein' such a sorry . . ."

Will caught himself just in time.

"Didn't mean no disrespect," he quickly interjected. "It's just that—"

"No, you can say it. I know the sorry old bastard he is."

Will was taken aback by her choice of terms. He had never heard a lady use such a word. But he supposed if anybody had the right to, Jessie did.

"Maybe somebody," he said, "will come along and take you out of all of this."

Again her cheeks gained color, and suddenly her head was down.

"I quit even dreaming that way," she whispered.

This time it was Will who couldn't look away, not when the sagging corners of her mouth begged for a reason to smile. He wanted to encourage her with a touch, but that wouldn't have been proper.

"Hope will carry you a long ways, Miss Jessie."

When she raised her eyes they seemed on the verge of welling up, and he thought he could see a tremble in her jaw. He didn't know what to make of her expression, and of course he couldn't see his own. But there must have been something striking about the way the two of them looked at each other, judging by what happened next.

"You got business with my Jessie?"

Will whirled. Caleb was in the doorway, fire in the deep scoring in his face as he clutched a skinned rabbit in one hand and a thirty-thirty in the other.

"Listen," said Will, "I—"

"He's just tending his friend," spoke up Jessie.

Caleb's hand tightened on the rifle, but it stayed low at his side. "Damned sure better be all he's tendin'."

Will was troubled by the suggestion of unseemly conduct on his part. He hoped Jessie didn't see it that way; she was the kind of girl worth courting.

"Git your butt outa here," slurred Caleb.

Will shifted his eyes back and forth between Caleb's scowl and Arch's drawn features before focusing on Arch.

"He needs water," he said determinedly, and then Jessie's fingers were close by, assisting as she had before. "I get finished up, I'll be goin'."

Will didn't know but what Caleb already was pulling down on him with the thirty-thirty, but he sure wasn't going to drag Arch out of all that water just to let him die for want of it.

"Soon's I can get back over with some men," he told Jessie, knowing her father was listening, "we'll carry him over to the wagon. Least, the storm quit blowin'."

"He doesn't need moving," said Jessie. "All that jostling."

Will glanced back at Caleb, who still stood scowling. "Not much choice."

"Sun will bake him," contended Jessie.

"Not in the shade."

"Shade doesn't stay one place. You'll be moving him all the time. I can look after him here."

Will looked around at Caleb.

"Don't mind him," Jessie whispered. And then to her father, "Papa—"

"You got chores," Caleb growled. "Git over here and start fryin' up this rabbit."

Will wanted to give Arch a little more water,

but he knew that he had stretched his luck too far already.

"Thank you, Miss Jessie," he said, handing her the cup. "Any change, we're camped in the mott. Wagon has a Slash Five burned in it."

He started for the door, and as he came even with Caleb he stopped and faced those crooked teeth and red-streaked eyes.

"I'll be sendin' a man over with some blankets for your daughter. Looks like you could use some flour and beans too."

Caleb continued to glower, but he didn't say no.

Putting on his hat, Will continued outside, but when he reached the step he couldn't keep from hesitating and looking back. With peripheral vision he could tell that Caleb still glared, but Will focused only on Jessie, whose gaze had followed him. Again he felt a strange and growing bond with this young woman he had only just met, and he tipped his hat.

"Miss Jessie," he said in departure.

Will hadn't gone a dozen steps from the house when he heard Caleb already berating and dominating. But what set Will's temples pounding was knowing that he couldn't do a damn thing about it.

Considering the look of suspicion that Quint had given him, Zeke would have fled in the night if not for the sandstorm.

But things had changed. Day had broken, and he had watched the Half Moon hand ride away with a Dove Creek-bound herd that cowhands had managed to hold together in a sheltered side canyon. Quint was sure to be gone an extended period, and that would give Zeke time to think about things. First, there was that strange darkness in Quint's face. If the Half Moon drover was wise to his part in Master Young's killing, what was the man waiting for? Second, Major Hyler had given Zeke the responsibility of recovering the Slash Five beeves, and how could he ever do it by taking flight?

He was tightening the cinch on a spirited brown, the horse as ready for the day's work as he was, when Will came walking up from the nester shack.

"Zeke," said Will, "Rayburn caught me a minute ago and wants me to look things over some more with him. I want you to hang around the wagon, case Miss Jessie—that nester girl—comes over about Arch."

"Yes, sir, Mister Will, but—"

"Arch would be dead, wasn't for you. He takes a turn for the worse, you got as much know-how as anybody."

"That man say he'd kill this colored person."

"You just do what you can and what you got to. He's like as not to be gone or passed out, anyhow. Oh, one more thing—get some flour and beans together, coffee, and take it on over. Arch's bedroll too. Just lay it on the step and you ought to not have any trouble."

No one had placed that kind of trust in Zeke since Master Young, and it made him feel good about himself for a change as he watched Will ride away. Still, the thought of venturing near that cabin with its hot-tempered tenant sent a shiver down Zeke's spine. He had been dodging an executioner of one kind or another all the way from the Big Red, and now that he was already on the Devils River it was just another six inches to hell.

Nevertheless, Zeke had never shirked a duty, so he threw the items across the front of his saddle as he would a dogie calf and rode up to the shack. He could smell wood smoke as it spiraled up from a flue. There was a hitching post at a corner, and he dismounted with trepidation and a wary eye. The odor of something cooking wafted through the partially open door, but from his angle he couldn't see anyone inside.

Against his better judgment, Zeke went ahead and secured his horse and started for the step with a sack of flour over his shoulder. He plopped it on the big rock and went back for another load, his spurs jingling with every step. He came back with dried beans and coffee, and just as he stacked them, the door swung open.

Petrified, he looked up expecting to see a

muzzle, but there was only the nester girl. He had noticed the day before that she was a mulatto like his mother, but she was light enough to have passed for white around most folks. He envied her, but he had no resentment.

"I be goin' soon's I get the rest."

He double-timed it to his horse and returned with a bedroll.

"You might wash it in boilin' water so's you don't get the lice. I be leavin' now."

"No use hurrying," said Jessie. "Papa's gone up the little canyon to sled some water back from the spring."

Zeke glanced toward the gulch and breathed a sigh of relief when he didn't see anyone.

"Mister Will told me, says, 'Zeke, you stay around the wagon so's you can help Miss Jessie, case Mister Arch do worse.' "

Something in her eyes suggested a moment of contemplation.

"Will Brite's awful thoughtful, looking after his man that way," she said. She nodded to the supplies. "For all of this too."

"Yes'm, Miss Jessie. Mister Will's funny sometimes, but he treat this colored person good."

"Funny?"

Jessie had caught Zeke thinking aloud; he knew it wasn't the kind of thing to tell a stranger.

"I don't mean it bad," he quickly explained, "just that he keep a lot to hisself."

Her head went down a moment. "He's got a gentle way I hadn't seen before. Papa—well, you know. Anybody that's mean to horses is mean to people too."

"Yes'm, I expects livin' here's like gettin' spurred in the shoulders ever' day."

"Will Brite says somebody will get me out of all this someday."

Zeke could see the longing in her expression.

"Yes'm, ever'body's gotta have somethin' to keep 'em goin', all right."

"What time he be back at the wagon?" she asked.

" 'Long about supper time, I reckon."

Jessie seemed to mull it over. "I'll be looking after Arch."

"Yes'm. You holler if you need somethin'."

He went to his horse, climbed on, and reined the animal toward camp.

"Zeke."

He held the bay and looked around to find her still framed in the doorway.

"You're awful gentle yourself," she said.

She was like a pretty sunrise standing there, and Zeke could have been smitten if not for all his still-powerful feelings for Vennie.

"Yes'm, figure we got somethin' in common. Least, some of our grandpappies did."

Just before sundown, with Arch resting peacefully and her father lost in a bottle as usual, Jessie slipped out the door and made her way down to the roundup camp in the oaks. She wandered from wagon to wagon, drawing considerable attention as she searched for one with a Slash Five on the side. Finally she spotted Zeke at a wagon under the great spreading limbs of a live oak. He was sitting on the tongue, and he had a tin plate, as did a near-dozen additional cowhands. The difference was, the other men—all of them white—sat or squatted together near the cook fire.

Jessie had been around cow camps enough to understand. A Negro or Mexican might be respected for his cowboying abilities, but when day's work was done he was expected to stay to himself or among his kind.

"Zeke."

Jessie came up from behind, across the tongue from the fire, and at the sound of her voice he turned and sprang to his feet.

"Somethin' bad, Miss Jessie?"

"He's resting easy enough." She looked over Zeke's shoulder at the huddled cowhands. "Will Brite come in?"

"No, ma'am, ain't—" Something behind her seized the Negro's attention. "Come somebody now, sure 'nough."

Jessie looked back into the sunset to see a silhouetted rider approaching with his horse in a gentle walk to avoid throwing dust over the cook fires. She couldn't distinguish his features, but when he came within forty yards, he veered toward her through the trees and quickened the animal's pace. Now she recognized him, and he pulled up before her and stepped off with his hat in his hand.

"Miss Jessie, you—"

"I spooned some broth down him," she interrupted, not wanting to alarm him. "He still hasn't woke up good."

Will's powdered face was as lathered as his mount, and he smelled the way a roundup hand should have. Still, he somehow exuded that peculiar hope, and suddenly there was no place she would rather have been than standing before him in this mosquito-infested cow camp.

"You offered her a plate, Zeke?" asked Will.

"I get her one," said the Negro, starting away.

"That's all right," spoke up Jessie. "I ate back at the house."

Zeke looked back and hesitated, and then perhaps sensing his place was elsewhere, he wandered away, digging into his supper.

"Somethin' I can do for you, Miss Jessie?" asked Will, subtly leading his horse away from the wagon.

Jessie followed at his side. "The flour and everything's a godsend."

"Least I can do for you takin' care of my man."

The gentle clomp of hoofs was the only sound for extended seconds, as though neither of them knew what to say. Then they circled behind a massive oak that hid them from camp, and Will held the bronc and faced her. Jessie stared into his squinty blue eyes for so long that her own must have bared every hidden corner of her soul.

"What you were saying this morning," she said. "About hope, how a body can hang on to dreams."

"You needin' some hope, aren't you, Miss Jessie."

She hung her head as all kinds of emotion stirred inside her. She found herself longing for an embrace that no good man would initiate so soon and no good woman could accept.

"Hope's somethin' I'm needin' too," Will added. "Keep your head up, Jessie."

The intimate use of her name without a courtesy title succeeded, and again she studied his eyes.

"Who are you, Will Brite?"

"Thought I said. Ride for the Slash Fives up on the Middle Concho."

"How come you so thoughtful? A name doesn't tell me who you are."

He looked a little quizzical. "Right now, I'd say I'm just a lucky hombre, standin' here talkin' to such a fine person."

"So where's home for you?"

Will nodded to the horse. "Back of one of them since I was thirteen."

"What about before?"

His face went solemn, and suddenly there was a lot of pain around his eyes.

"Zeke says you keep some things bottled up," she added when he didn't answer.

He wiped his sweaty brow as he looked away.

"Zeke ought not talk so much," he said.

"That why you're needing hope too? The things you keep inside?"

Now he faced her again, this time with a forced smile.

"I swan, Jessie, even the boss man don't ask so many questions. But I think I'd crawl through a cactus patch just to hear you ask them."

"You make fun of your girl back home that way?"

"What girl? You been listenin' to Zeke again? I'm off chasin' cows all day and he's here talkin' up a storm to a pretty girl."

"You really think so?"

"That he was here talkin'?"

"Now you *are* making fun of me, Will Brite."

"Well, I don't know much else to do."

"You could let me see you crawl through that cactus patch. I could walk along hollering *gee!* and *haw!* and ply you with questions."

The grimness in Will's face was all gone now, replaced by laugh lines.

"Now who's makin' fun?" he asked.

The playful banter went on for several more minutes, and Jessie couldn't remember ever having so much fun. She didn't know how she found it in herself to muster even a smile, much less a laugh. But here she stood, giggling like a schoolgirl with a man she hadn't known existed until the day before.

Then reality set in.

"How long you going to be here?" she asked.

"On the Devils? Till roundup's done. We got a booger we're dealin' with."

"You come to the house some more?"

"Your father run me out once already. But I'll do what I got to to look in on my man."

Jessie felt crestfallen, and abruptly all she could see was Will's dusty boot.

"To see you too, Jessie," he added.

Lying in his bedroll at Beaver Lake on previous nights, Will had looked up at the stars between the oak leaves and wondered if any of those screaming Negro children had found a place among them. But stretched out on this evening, he saw only the enchanting eyes and dainty, square chin of a young woman. For years, he had lived under a suffocating shadow that had denied hope, but this daughter of a nester drunkard had already buoyed his spirits in a mere three visits.

Jessie.

Was she his own "Sweet Mary" who could rescue him from so dark a past? Or did he even have the right, considering that he had come to accept—even embrace—the cloud of judgment hanging over him?

Still, the memory of her sparkling eyes and good-natured teasing wouldn't go away. Somehow she kindled a part of him that had forgotten how to live. It was a mere spark, all right, but it was there, ready to flare and carry him to places he had never dreamed.

Over the next several days, Jessie saw Will repeatedly when he came to the cabin to check on Arch, something he did only when her father's horse was gone from the nearby trap. She supposed Will's discretion was for the best, considering their growing friendship and Caleb's controlling nature, but she longed to see him more.

When Will failed to show up one evening

despite her father's absence, she walked to the Slash Five camp and found only the cook. Returning disappointed, she stepped inside the cabin, only to have Caleb seize her arm.

"Where the hell you been?" Liquor was powerful on his breath.

"Papa, you're hurting me."

Caleb only dug his nails deeper and swigged from a bottle.

"Said, where you been?"

She tried to pry his hand away. "Down by the lake. Now turn me loose."

Caleb's bloodshot eyes burned like fires. "Been with that cowhand, ain't ya? You better tell me, girl!"

Jessie did her best to squirm free. "That's none of your business."

"You stay away from him, you hear me? I got things for you to do."

"You don't own me."

He twisted her arm. "You'll do as I say! You gonna respect me."

Jessie had seen the same wild and threatening look in his face so many times, but he was beyond respecting.

"You mean old bastard!" she cried, still clawing at his hold.

Now he did turn her loose, but the next thing she knew, the back of his gnarled hand came up hard against her mouth and cheekbone. Reeling, she went down, but she had no more than hit the floor than something jerked her head. She tried to cover up as he dragged her by the hair, but she took two or three more blows before he was through.

Hurting and tasting blood, Jessie looked up through white specks to see him scowling.

"Nothin' but a whore chases after a man that way!" he yelled. "A whore like your mama! That's what you is—a whore like her! You stay away from him!"

Caleb paused long enough to take another drink. "Now get up and fix me some supper."

He began staggering away toward his bed, but Jessie did no more than come up to one hand and glare after him.

"You beat her too, didn't you, Papa. You treated her like dirt, or else she wouldn't had reason to find somebody else."

Caleb whirled off-balance, the lamplight throwing a shadow as ominous as his enraged face.

"I'll beat the whorin' outa you, you little—"

Caleb stumbled and fell hard, the bottle clanging down beside him and splattering whiskey across the plank floor. He sprawled there, a wretch of a man, stunned or passed out—Jessie wasn't sure which. Either way, she would be ready.

Coming to her feet, she touched the back of her

hand to her lip, finding the blood she knew would be there, and went to the shelf. The revolver lay shining in the lamplight, its grip beckoning. She hesitated, studying the curvature of its cylinder, the caked rust along the barrel, the hammer waiting to be cocked.

Caleb had neglected and abused her time and again over the years, and she had always cowered and borne it. But that had been before Will Brite, before hope, and now that she had tasted it, she would do the unthinkable rather than give it up.

Jessie took the weapon, finding it strangely heavy, and her thumb was already on the hammer as she turned to Caleb. He had gained enough awareness to stretch out his fingers, sopping the spilled liquor and tasting it. He looked so pitiful that she almost felt sorry for him, and then her burning face and all the punishing memories brought her thumbing the hammer back.

The cylinder turned, locking the trigger into place. The latter's quarter moon shape grew smooth and firm against her forefinger as she brought the barrel swinging across coal oil lamp and table leg to the evil man still sopping whiskey.

She could do it right now. She could squeeze the trigger and hear the roar, and blood would pool beside the liquor. She could do it and no one would think the worse of her, not the law or Will Brite or—

Will Brite.

What would he think of a girl who had killed her own father? Could anything be any more unnatural, no matter the justification? Would she destroy her newfound hope by the very act with which she was trying to save it?

She still hovered between conviction and doubt when she heard an unfamiliar voice from behind.

"Thirst . . . supreme thirst . . ."

Jessie turned, finding the injured Slash Five hand tossing and muttering feverishly. With a measure of relief, she replaced the weapon on the shelf. Arch's words had been the first that she was able to recognize, and as she dipped a cup of water and went to him, she took it as a sign that good things could still happen.

Fresh blood had collected in the cowhand's ear, and she dabbed it with a rag before raising his head and tilting the cup to his lips.

"Brought you water," she said.

He was unresponsive at first, his eyes still closed, but as the water ran between his lips he brought up both hands, bumping her arm and spilling a little in his blind grope.

"Here," she said, guiding the cup into his fingers.

Jessie maintained a hold, but Arch did his part too, as well as with an additional cupful. He was semiconscious at best, but she spoke to him throughout, trying to reach a part of him that the horse hadn't addled.

"I'm Jessie. They tell me your name's Arch. You've been hurt, but you're getting better. You're going to rest easy here till you get well."

She glanced over her shoulder and found Caleb passed out again.

"Will Brite's coming to see you, soon as he can," she continued, now that she didn't have to be restrained in what she said. "I wish you could tell me about him—his favorite color, all his likes, the things he keeps to himself. I wish you could tell me what he thinks of me, if . . . if he might take me away from all this some-time."

Maybe Jessie was just vulnerable. Maybe lasting relationships couldn't spring from a whirlwind of emotions and events. Maybe in her desperation she had built up everything so much that reality couldn't match it. All she knew was that she saw in Will the only chance she had ever had for a tomorrow.

She left Caleb where he lay drooling, and from a box under Arch's cot she pulled out her most prized possession. It was her mother's leather-bound Bible, or so said the name in front, and she had managed to keep it secreted away all these years. The dog-eared pages were scorched, but they were all there, just as she had rescued them when Caleb, in a drunken fit, had piled her mother's belongings and set them afire. Everything else had burned, but he had staggered away and left her to dig in the coals and find a treasure.

Dragging the lamp closer, Jessie sat on the floor and leaned back against a table leg so that the glow illuminated the pages. This Bible was her sole material connection to someone buried for long years, and when whiskey would fog Caleb's head, she would often thumb through and long to know the mother who had died giving her life. There were so many things about her that Jessie wanted to find out from Caleb, but the best she could do was read again all the passages marked by her mother's hand. They had touched her mother's heart, and across time and distance they touched Jessie's, too.

Jessie's eyes fell on a bracketed passage that spoke to her in a voice silenced the moment she had been born.

In the world ye shall have tribulation.

Jessie supposed that no matter the troubles she had known, her mother's had been just as trying. It was something the two of them shared, this abuse at the hands of a controlling man, and tonight the realization seemed to bond them more than ever before.

Jessie read on.

But be of good cheer; I have overcome the world.

Her mother must have believed it; otherwise, she wouldn't have marked it. Jessie wanted to believe it too, but to find cheer in knowing that Caleb would take away all her tomorrows seemed impossible.

The pages went fuzzy, and Jessie clutched her mother's Bible to her breast and wept for all the things she would never have.

19

After work responsibilities deprived Will of his evening visit to the line shack, he couldn't wait for the next day and another chance to see Jessie. Nevertheless, by the time he helped throw two thousand beeves together for another drive north, it was already late morning.

A rising gray plume and the smell of wood smoke drew Will and his horse to the rear of the shack. Jessie was there, her head down as she stirred a large cast iron pot with a stick. Steam rose to the pop of the fire as he pulled rein several yards shy to keep the dust down.

"Mornin', Jessie."

When she didn't acknowledge him with even a glance, Will folded his hands across the saddle horn and studied her—the apron ruffling in the wind, the shadow of the flue darkening her shoulders, the dust caking a scuffed pair of boots a couple of sizes too big. Women had always been as much a mystery to Will as tomorrow was, so he didn't know what to make of her demeanor.

Stepping off his horse, he tied it to a mesquite bush under the eave of the house and started toward her. She had to know that he approached, but she nevertheless kept her face turned.

"What's the matter, Jessie?"

She shrugged and made a half-hearted attempt to agitate the pot's contents.

"Can't . . . Fire won't get . . . Can't get it hot enough." A lot seemed to hang in her throat.

Will looked her over again. "I remember my mama—the other Jessie—washin' clothes the same way. Here, let me throw a little more wood on."

The fire looked plenty hot to Will, the way the water rolled and gurgled, but he went ahead and gathered a few mesquite limbs from the pile at Jessie's left. He was in front of her now, and as he knelt to stoke the fire, he looked up and saw her purple-bruised face and swollen lip.

Startled, he let the wood fall, and burst to his feet.

"What happened to your face?"

This time, Jessie didn't try to hide anything—not the bruising or swelling or her red and welling eyes.

"I . . . I don't think I . . . I can't see you anymore."

He barely heard her words, so powerful an image was her beaten face.

"He do this to you? I'll tear him apart!"

He whirled to the empty trap, and then turned back at the touch of Jessie's hand.

"He rode out before I woke up, took the flour you gave us. Probably going to the railroad to trade it for liquor."

Will's rage continued to build. "I'll ride him down if you want me to. I'll grab a fresh horse and ride the bastard down!"

Too late, Will realized he had breached the cowboy code of conduct that required that he curb his language around women. Ashamed, he removed his hat and held it penitently on his chest with both hands.

"I'm sorry, Jessie. It slipped out and it shouldn't have. What would you like me to do?"

She seemed to look deep inside him with her puffy eyes. "Hold me, Will Brite."

He ran a gentle thumb along the bruise at her cheek. "You poor thing."

He slipped gentle arms around her for the first time and felt her tremble. In that moment, it struck him how much he cared for her, this nester girl he had met so recently. The connection was stronger than anything he had ever known, and the power and suddenness of it scared him a little.

He grew aware of her soft hair against his cheek, and even more so of the warmth of her curves.

"You deserve to be treated better, Jessie," he said.

She pulled away just far enough to show her questioning eyes. "*You* treat me good."

It was as if a dark cloud abruptly swept over everything, reminding Will of the penance he served.

"You deserve better than me," he whispered, withdrawing and turning away.

"How come you say that?" she pressed. "You're so caring."

Yeah, he thought, *as carin' as hell's goin' to be with me.*

He felt her hands on his shoulders and he wanted to face her. He wanted to sweep her up in his arms again and forget all the things he was powerless to change.

"You don't know me, Jessie, the things I've done."

"I know you're thoughtful. Gentle. I don't think I knew what either one of those was till you."

A lot of things churned inside Will, but he felt sudden shame that he had made this all about him for a moment instead of Jessie.

"You didn't tell me," he said, turning. "What you want me to do."

A frightful sense of loss seemed to grip her words.

"Like you did before, Will Brite. Hold me so I can remember."

Will had never seen anyone so in need of an

embrace, so in need of hope, but she had more to say.

"Papa comes back, I . . ."

"He say somethin' about me? He say you couldn't see me no more?"

Jessie's words wouldn't come, but he didn't have to hear them; they were written too clearly on her face. It was one thing for Will, of his own volition, to deny himself a chance to be happy, but it was another thing entirely for someone else to do it, and a part of him long dead seemed to come alive again.

He put his hands on her shoulders.

"I'll hold you, Jessie, and when I come back, I'll keep on holdin' you long as you want me to."

Giving her a quick hug, he mounted up and rode away to the sound of his name on her lips.

Zeke's eyes were on the roundup herd, but his mind was on faraway Quint and what that Half Moon cowboy might suspect about him.

It was afternoon near Beaver Lake, and Zeke slowly rode a circle, helping two other cowhands contain all the crow-bait beeves. He couldn't believe the blizzard of winter had given way to such strength-sapping heat, but at least the sun didn't eat away his flesh the way the snow had done. The pain in his foot still shot all the way up his leg every time he stepped up in the saddle.

He wondered what kind of pain he would feel when he planted a boot on the gallows.

In imagination, Zeke already had the hangman's knot under his ear when he heard someone calling his name. He turned with a squeak of leather to see Jessie approaching across the dusty bottom that stretched several hundred yards to the nester cabin.

Zeke glanced at the cattle, assuring himself that the other two men had them under control, and then broke off his circuit and loped his horse out to meet her. He was troubled to find her face puffy and badly bruised, with worry lines that nobody but him should have. Still, his first concern was for his fellow cowhand.

"It Mister Arch, Miss Jessie?" he asked, pulling up before her.

"You've got to do something for me, Zeke." There was urgency in her voice.

"Yes'm."

From under her wind-blown apron, she withdrew a glinting revolver and extended it grip-first.

"Will Brite headed out for the railroad after Papa. I didn't know the old devil had took his rifle, but it's not there."

Zeke hesitated. The last time he had touched a six-shooter a man had died.

"How come Mister Will needin' a gun?"

Jessie didn't answer, but Zeke saw the answer

in her battered face. Back on the plantation a straw boss had once horse-whipped young Zeke; when Master Young had found out, he had ordered the man off the place at gunpoint.

Jessie pushed the forty-five into Zeke's hand, and he had no choice but to take it.

"You've got to hurry!" she urged.

Zeke glanced over his shoulder at the beeves. Even night-herding seldom required more than the two drovers already giving duty, and as weak as these cattle were, they were in no danger of running. Nevertheless, Zeke was reluctant.

"Mister Will say hold them cows."

"He doesn't know Papa's got a rifle! Don't you understand?"

Zeke understood, all right. Somebody was liable to get killed over this, and if that was the case, one look at Jessie's beaten face told him who it should be.

With a quick "I be gone!" Zeke spurred his animal toward the remuda and a fresh horse that would take him farther down the devil's trail.

Zeke didn't know how much of a head start Will had, or how far he would have to ride before this was over, so he varied his roan's gait between a jog-trot and a walk. Dead cattle tolled off the miles, the reek sickening his stomach. This was the first time he had ridden down-canyon, and with every bend the carcasses and blowing flies grew thicker. Zeke had heard men call the Pecos the graveyard of the cowman's hopes, but he figured it had only been because they hadn't seen the Devils this spring of eighty-five.

He passed water holes floating with putrid carrion, scared up vulture after feeding vulture, came upon staggering beeves and others already down and too far gone to tail up. Even when he reached the Devils' living water and the woods surrounded him, the gloom only added to the atmosphere of despair.

This was a trail of death, and the six-shooter in his waistband was primed to add to it.

At sundown Zeke rode past the old fort, the silhouetted walls rising like tombstones over a boneyard. When the main canyon bent east a short distance beyond, he kept to the road that tracked south up another long canyon. The roan climbed steadily, leaving the wooded bottom-land far below as yucca and daggered bear grass began to crowd close on either side.

Zeke held his course on into nightfall, guided by the roan's night vision. About an hour beyond the fort he topped out on a rolling divide with eerie yucca standing guard in the starlight. It was a lonely place, the silence pierced only by the gelding's hoofbeats and the forlorn yelping of coyotes.

A couple of tiresome hours out of the Devils' valley, an imposing shadow rose up across

Zeke's path. Its rugged outline against starry sky told him it was a line of one-hundred-foot hills, broken directly ahead by a narrow pass. He had heard somebody tell of a gap in these parts called Dead Man's, named for some long-ago Indian massacre. He figured this had to be the place, for he couldn't imagine any location more somber by night.

Forty yards shy of the pass, Zeke came abreast of an indistinguishable shadow on his right. It stirred strangely, boogering his bronc, but all he could see was a shifting mass that blended in with a low ridge two hundred yards beyond.

"You there, Mister Will?" he asked, steadying the roan.

For a moment, there was only the hollow play of his voice against the hills, and then came confused words.

"Zeke? What the hell you doin' here, Zeke?"

Will began to take shape, a faceless form standing beside a horse.

"I come after you. Miss Jessie sent me."

"Jessie? How come?"

"She 'fraid for you, Mister Will. She say her papa take a rifle. She say bring you a six-shooter."

"A six-shooter? You bring it?"

Zeke extended it in the dark. "You reach out, you find it."

Zeke groped blindly before their hands

connected long enough to make the exchange. For almost a minute thereafter, Will stayed silent.

"I'm not likin' this, I tell you," Will finally allowed.

"Bad seein' Miss Jessie thataway, all right."

"Yeah. If there was ever anybody needin' killin' . . ."

Will's words roused all the unforgivable memories that blackened Zeke's soul, and even though the night retained the stifling heat of day, he began to shiver.

Dismounting, Zeke stepped around the nose of his horse so he could stand face to face with Will in the gloom. Zeke knew that what he had to say was outside a colored man's place, but there were some things worth violating the accepted code of conduct.

"Killin' a man's a awful thing, Mister Will."

Will fell silent for longer than Zeke expected, and when he responded, there was a strange, probing note in his voice.

"What would you know about killin', Zeke?"

Now it was Zeke who didn't want to talk, and he was glad Will couldn't see his face. Hell had to be written all over it.

"I . . . I just knows it do bad things to you insides. It take all the light out of a man's soul."

For long seconds, only a distant lobo had anything to say, and Zeke could only imagine Will's turmoil.

"Somethin's got to be done," Will finally said. "I don't want to have to kill nobody, especially not her daddy. All I want's to turn around and ride on back. But somethin's got to be done."

"If that man got a gun," said Zeke, "he ain't gonna stand for no whippin' to be put on him. You catch up, they's gonna be shootin', and where they's shootin', that ol' graveyard be a-waitin'."

"So what the hell I'm supposed to do? If I'm any kind of man, I can't just let him beat her that way."

"Mister Will, I expect he been beatin' Miss Jessie her whole life, same's they beat her grandpappies and my grandpappies."

"What's that mean?" asked Will.

It had never occurred to Zeke that Will didn't realize that Jessie was a mulatto, with the same kind of slave blood that Zeke carried. Maybe it was too much to have expected, considering Jessie's features. Regardless, Will didn't need anything else rolling around in his mind right now.

"Who been beatin' whose grandfathers?" pressed Will.

"That man, he a mean one," said Zeke. "If he be able to ride back, get the idea Miss Jessie sic you on him, he beat her even worse."

Zeke couldn't tell for sure, but Will appeared to turn away with a wag of his head as he muttered a quick "Hell!"

"So it's all or nothin' then," Will went on. "I either kill the SOB or I turn around right now."

No matter what Zeke had said, he knew what he would do. If it was his sweet Vennie all puffy and bruised, he knew what he would do.

"I reckon," said Zeke, "all depend on what Miss Jessie mean to you."

Will's shadow turned back to Zeke. "She's a woman. Any man with self-respect, that ought to be the only reason he needs. But *killin'* . . . It eats away at a body, all right, just like you say."

Now it was the wagon boss who talked as if he knew something about killing, and Zeke wondered if Will's secrets were as dark as his own.

"Maybe you oughta roll you a smoke, Mister Will. A smoke always makes this colored person think a little better."

He didn't know what Will did, but Zeke went ahead and dug out his muslin sack and blindly tried to sprinkle a little tobacco on a sheet of paper. He didn't know if he had rolled a cigarette or empty paper until he tasted it as he licked and sealed it. Cupping a flaring match to his mouth, he lighted the butt with a quick puff.

The moment he lowered his hands, something screamed past his ear to a reverberating blast.

"What the—!"

Startled as much as his horse, Zeke barely

heard Will's cry as his grip on the reins jerked him away from a second whizzing shot.

"Plottin' to kill me, are ya!" someone shouted from all too close.

"Get that cigarette out!" cried Will.

Ducking, Zeke got rid of the butt, but it wasn't enough. All around the glowing ember, the gravel began to burst to more gunfire, scourging his shins.

Zeke ran, tugging at his terrified pony. Maybe Jessie's father couldn't see any better than Zeke, but that didn't mean much the way the slugs splattered left and right, front and back.

"Pot-shottin' us!" yelled Will. "Got to fight him off!"

The next thing Zeke heard was the roar of Will's six-shooter, followed by a second report, and four more. Then there was nothing but the rattle of the saddle as Zeke desperately swung astride his horse.

"You on?" shouted Will.

"We gotta ride, Mister Will!" answered Zeke, touching spurs to hide.

Two sets of hoofs counted out a frantic cadence as the roan flew back up-trail through the night. Any second a bullet could have exploded into Zeke's back, but all he could do was hug the roan's neck and beg the animal for greater speed. It was bad enough getting shot at for the first time in his life, but blind flight from a slug he couldn't outrace was enough to test the mettle of even a man who figured a bullet was what he deserved.

The two horses raced side-by-side a half-mile before Zeke reined up at a word from Will. Whirling the roan, the Negro found only the outline of Dead Man's Pass against a jeweled sky.

"Black as pitch!" said Will. "Can't hear nothin'—you?"

"Mean man ain't a-followin', sure 'nough ain't."

"Jessie give you more bullets?"

"She just puts ol' six-gun in my hand and say ride."

"I was snappin' against empty before it was over. Sure shut up that rifle of his, though. You don't suppose I hit him?"

With the last question, fear took hold of his words, and it was a distraught man who continued.

"Good God, I-I can't be killing her father. I-I don't care what he done, it's not right, just not right. How could I go look her in the eyes and tell—"

"She say, 'Take gun to Mister Will,' " repeated Zeke. " 'Hurry,' she say. Miss Jessie got no worries for her pappy, just for you."

"Still . . ."

"She like my Vennie is to me, ain't she, Mister

227

Will? Anyways, don't reckon how you could've hit him, dark so thick you could cut it with a knife."

Will seemed to contemplate that as Zeke stared back at Dead Man's Pass.

"I just can't ride off without knowin', bein' able to tell her somethin'," said Will. "We got to hang around till daylight and find out."

"Don't forget, you out of bullets," reminded Zeke. "He get us in his sights, liable to blow our heads off."

"Did his best to, that's for damned sure. Zeke, this isn't your fight. You can go on back if you're a mind, and I won't hold it against you."

"You better come too, Mister Will."

"If I was smart, guess I would. But sometimes you just got to listen to what's inside you."

Abruptly Zeke's insides had plenty to tell him, and he had no choice but to pay attention. By sunrise, he could be back at the wagon, living every moment in regret for more reasons than he could count, or he might be dead. He didn't figure one could be any worse than the other.

"Guess I be a-stayin' too."

20

Even with a star-studded sky, Will had never known a night so black. It seemed to reach deep in his soul, summoning up added remorse for what he may have done to Jessie's father.

Why it should have bothered him so, he didn't understand, but he dwelled on it as he and Zeke retreated another couple of miles from Dead Man's Pass and then veered off-trail.

He led the way west across rocky desert for several minutes before they stopped and staked their horses in a flat crowded with big yucca. Ideally, they should have unsaddled the broncs, but with Caleb maybe still out there with a rifle, all they could afford to do was remove the bridles so the animals could graze what nubs they might find.

"Can't both doze off at once," said Will. "You go ahead and sleep a little first."

"Good Lord might put a whippin' on me for sayin', but I wishin' the gravedigger was already throwin' dirt in that mean man's face. Got it comin', he do."

Suddenly Will could see Jessie's face, vivid and swollen. But he also could see those Texarkana flames torching the night. "Suppose any of us get what we deserve?" he asked.

Now Zeke went quiet, the yelping of coyotes tolling off the seconds before he answered.

"If Boss Man make you live with what I do ever' day—and Him still a-wantin' more—I figure we won't ever pay enough."

Will shuddered. With the sudden new life he had discovered through Jessie, he had somehow managed to hide things from himself for a while. But now he saw what a lie he had been living the past few days. He was just another screwworm maggot eating away at what little good there was in the world, and he abruptly understood something that he wished he didn't.

As heinous an act as Caleb's had been, it was nothing compared to what a ten-year-old boy had done. If Caleb deserved killing by someone like him, then Will's own punishment had to lie deeper in the bowels of hell than Lucifer himself.

"So no way, you think, we can ever be forgive for things?" Will asked.

"I asks myself that all time, I do. The Man that died on that cross mighty big on forgiveness, they say, but I wonders."

Will hung his head. "He don't know what I done."

"I expect He do, Mister Will."

Will looked up at Zeke's shadowy face, and on up at the stars flung so silent and lonely across the sky. Could anybody out there really give a damn about somebody like him?

His voice went hoarse. "Search the whole world over, and the sky too, and I reckon there won't be enough forgiveness to wipe my slate clean."

"Must be awful bad what you done, just like this colored person."

Will wished he could see Zeke's eyes in the dark. For days, ever since Quint of the Half Moons had tipped him off, Will had quietly taken note of Zeke. He wanted to ask him straight out if he was the Negro who had shot and robbed the Half Moon owner. Everything about him kept pointing to it, but Will knew this wasn't the time for probing, not when Zeke had volunteered to join him in going up against an armed man just because it was the right thing to do.

Or maybe Will wasn't the only one whose desire to live blew with the winds of emotion.

Flour-dusted ground. Pitted by dark stains in daybreak's subdued light.

Will and Zeke had approached the hollow from behind the cacti-strewn ridge on the west, and now they held their mounts among the desert succulents that dotted the land all the way

231

to the road and mouth of Dead Man's Pass. The blood trail began under a yucca at a sack of flour—the cloth ripped by thorn or gunfire—and continued a few yards toward the gap before seemingly disappearing.

"Blood just a-drip-drippin'," said Zeke, "but mean man climbed on his horse, he done."

"I . . . I didn't think I could've hit him," said a troubled Will as he studied the blood. "Maybe . . . Maybe he ought to shot me too."

When he looked up, he found Zeke staring at him.

"No use wishin' down punishment," said the Negro. "Lord A'mighty deal out plenty on us all by Hisself."

Will continued to dwell on the blood. "Think he's dyin'?"

"Don't know where you hit him." Zeke turned and surveyed Dead Man's Pass. "If he still out there, he dangerous like a wounded panther, only he got more than teeth and claws to fight with. Nothin' we need to tangle with."

Suddenly Will had all kinds of concern for Jessie. "We got to make sure he went through that pass, didn't turn back for Beaver Lake."

With a sense of urgency, Will took his bay to the point where the dark stains ended, leaned over to identify the onward-threading horse tracks, and began to trace them. The upside-down U's led him past bear grass, tasajillo, and prickly pear to a point on the road twenty yards shy of Dead Man's. The turf here was easier to read, and just as Will drew rein, Zeke pulled up alongside and pointed to the dirt.

"Still a-bleedin' out," said Zeke. Then he lifted his arm. "See yonder? Headed right 'twixt them mountains."

Will looked for himself. For a quarter-mile, rugged, cacti-infested hills hovered over the road on both sides—a gateway for the dead of yesteryear and maybe the dying of the night before.

"I hate to think I shot somebody," he said quietly. "But I hope to God he don't ever come ridin' back through there."

"Go awful bad if he do," said Zeke. "He add ever'thing up, don't see how he keep from killin' poor Miss."

Will knew it too, just as he remained aware of the promise he had made to Jessie just prior to riding away. But that had been before he had realized again that somebody like him could never be worthy of her or any other decent woman, no matter how much he might wish it.

It was a hard ride back to Beaver Lake, and Will dozed off in the saddle more than once before all the wagons in the big oak mott came into view. While Zeke continued on for the Slash Five camp, Will veered his bay for the nester shack.

From inside the open door, Jessie must have

seen him riding up, because she came running out before he reached the hitching post.

"Don't you leave me that way anymore, Will Brite."

Her flushed face, her red eyes, the tone of her voice—everything about her spoke of anger mixed with grave concern. Will didn't know how to respond so he said nothing at all, but the moment he stepped off his horse Jessie was there, clinging to him.

He embraced her tentatively, remembering once more the reasons he could never have her, even as her distraught words continued to come.

"When I found the rifle gone . . . How could you go off that way!" Then she pulled back far enough for him to see her eyes. "Did you find him? What—"

"Caught up with him, place they call Dead Man's. Went to shootin' at us in the dark. Had to sh—" He shook his head. "Didn't have no choice—I shot back, give us time to get out of there."

"In the dark? Then you didn't hit . . ."

Will gripped her firmly by the shoulders, bracing for what was to come.

"I shot him, Jessie. I don't know how, but . . ."

It was a hell of a thing, telling her something like that, and he looked down for a moment to regain his composure. He still couldn't find words, but Jessie did.

"You killed him, didn't you." Her eyes were wide and staring but expressionless.

"No. Least, I don't think so. Found his trail this mornin', headin' on south. He was bleedin' a awful lot."

Jessie may have held her emotions in check, but Will could not, and it showed in his choked voice.

"Lord, I-I'm sorry, Jessie!"

A darkness came over her features. "I'm just sorry he was able to ride away."

Will was so shocked that such a statement could have come from her that all he could do was stare. But as he looked, he focused for the first time today on her and not himself, and he didn't like what he saw. Her bruises were worse, a deathly blue, almost black, that spread across half her swollen face. Her lip was no longer as puffy, but now it showed a vertical cut that wouldn't close. Worst of all, her jaw had ballooned, casting her face into a grotesque misrepresentation of the pretty girl he knew her to be.

"Good God, Jessie," he muttered. "Good God, what he done to you!"

Her eyes began to well. When a tear crept down her cheek, forming a glistening stream against the discoloration, he wiped it away with a gentle thumb.

"All I see's the bruises," he whispered. "I can't

see what he's done to you inside all these years."

"He'll be back," she managed, "and it'll be just like before. Only worse."

"I'm not goin' to let that happen. I swear I won't, Jessie." He looked at the open door. "How's Arch?'

"Still in and out of it. Mostly out, but he's quit bleeding at the ear."

Will turned and studied the smoke rising from all the cook fires in the live oaks beside the lake.

"I'll get some men and move him over to the wagon. You too."

Will felt Jessie's hands on his chest, drawing his attention back to her.

"You'll be going back," she said quietly. "One of these days you'll be leaving for the Concho."

Will knew the question she was posing, the fruits of his impulsive promise to her. He was a cowhand, and to a cowhand, a promise was a sacred pact not to be broken. But right now he felt less an honorable cowboy than a scratch-blowing screwworm fly.

"Tell me something, Will Brite. Tell me."

He told her the only thing he could.

"Go get your things together. I'll be back with some men to help with Arch soon's I can."

Will didn't know how he had gotten himself into such a fix.

Earlier in the month he'd had a responsibility to Arch, and he had done what had been necessary to take care of him. But in doing so, he had tangled himself in the personal affairs of a couple of nesters and couldn't find a way out.

Will flinched as the thought bounced around in his head. Was that all Jessie was to him? A nester girl causing him all kinds of trouble?

Maybe he wished it were that way. Maybe the ten-year-old boy in him who searched for punishment wished it more than anything. But the man he had become—the man who had held Jessie and looked into her eyes—knew better. Even this quickly, he had come to care about her in a way he never had anybody else.

That was why he sat alone in the brush, his night horse staked nearby, and watched the starlit valley in its gentle bend from west to south. To his left, a mere fifty yards, the shack was a dark shadow waiting, as he did, for the return of a soul as dark as Will's own.

Since nightfall Will had been here, denying himself precious sleep just so he would know if Caleb came back. Over at the Slash Five camp, Jessie and the whole outfit were no doubt asleep, and Will didn't want him sneaking up with a thirty-thirty ready for vengeance.

For the dozenth time, Will tested the balance of Jessie's six-shooter and found it increasingly heavy. He hoped to God Caleb wouldn't show up, because he didn't know what to do if he did. Will was a cowhand, not a lawman, and even if he could keep a steady hand while his heart hammered, he doubted he could hit the broad side of a barn.

Yet a wild shot in the gloom had somehow found its mark, and he continued to have mixed feelings about it.

Just as the sky began to glow orange in the east, a shadowy form slowly came nodding up the valley and veered toward the line shack. Its gait suggested a horse, not a cow, and Will's jaw tightened at the same time that his hand did on the revolver grip.

Will jumped to his feet, alarming his bronc a little, and edged a little deeper in the brush. There was safety in concealment, but his pulse nevertheless quickened and his mouth went dry as he watched the figure's deliberate approach.

God Almighty, one shootout a lifetime was more than most cowboys ever experienced, and here he was on the verge of two in successive nights. He didn't know whether to start shooting as wildly as before, or shout a challenge that would bring that rifle swinging toward him. The first choice would have been potential murder, the second, likely suicide, so Will decided to wait and watch.

The horse had already halted at the shack before Will realized the saddle was empty.

Stunned, Will just stared for long seconds, and then with soft words to the animal, he parted the thorny limbs at his face and began to approach. Seldom could a cowhand walk right up to a skittish bronc, but the foamy roan was so jaded that Will had little trouble taking the reins.

There was dark discoloration along the skirt of the saddle and down the fender, as though somebody had spilled a bucket of paint. But not until he turned the horse to inspect things by the light of breaking day did he realize it was dried blood.

Will looked up across the bronc's withers to the trail leading down-canyon to Dead Man's Pass and beyond. His initial sense of relief gave way to crushing guilt spanning two decades. A man had died out there, by Will's own hand, but maybe it would have been more just if two men had died.

Will figured he must have been the biggest coward in the world.

It didn't matter that he could climb back on a sunfishing bronc that had just thrown him, or unflinchingly gig his mount through a midnight stampede across prairie dog holes waiting to break his neck. Nothing in a cowboy's world, absolutely nothing, required the degree of courage he needed to tell Jessie that he had killed the man who had given her life.

But hadn't that same man also dragged her through hell?

He found Jessie placing her dirty breakfast dishes in the roundup pan at the wagon. Around her, camp was a beehive of activity as cowhands readied for the day's work.

"Jessie," he said as he approached from behind, "I got to talk to you."

She obviously hadn't realized he was in camp, for surprise was in her face as she turned.

"You're here," she said. "Nobody knew what came of you last night."

Will didn't like looking in her eyes. He took her arm and nodded to the oaks past the campfire.

"Let's go over here somewhere."

"What is it?" she asked.

Will didn't answer as he escorted her through the drifting smoke toward the rising sun, fleeting brightness through all the low-hanging limbs. He could have taken her into the trees nearer the lake, but he had good memories of their talk there and he wanted to keep them that way. There were plenty of twisted live oaks ahead, and when the two of them reached a secluded spot with intertwined limbs above and a wall of underbrush all around, he stopped and took her hands. Still he couldn't bring himself to look at her.

"I-I hate tellin' you this, Jessie. You don't know how much I hate it."

"It's him, isn't it? Just say what you have to, Will Brite."

With willpower he didn't think he had, he brought his gaze up. "His horse come back."

"What does . . . ? Where . . . ?"

"Blood. A whole bucketful, like it was poured on that saddle. Nobody can lose that much."

"He's dead? That's what you're tell—"

"I am, Jessie. God forgive me, I-I am."

He couldn't read her expression at first, but she came closer, obviously needing a hug he felt he had no right to give. When he hesitated, she laid her head against his chest and embraced him nonetheless.

"You said you'd hold me," she whispered.

There still seemed something wrong about trying to comfort her under the circumstances, but he allowed her inside his arms. She began to quake, and he suspected that she was silently sobbing.

"I . . . I should've let him go," he said hoarsely, surprised at how deeply the news affected her. "I should've, but I just couldn't let him keep hittin' you. If I'd knowed how much you thought of him—"

Abruptly she pulled away, showing a face racked by emotion.

"Listen to me, Will Brite. I'm not crying for what I lost. I'm crying for what I never did have."

Will couldn't understand, and it must have shown in his expression and silence.

She went on. "Even if he'd been my real father—"

"He wasn't?"

Jessie wouldn't be interrupted. "Just raising me wouldn't've been enough anyway. I never had a father. Mother either. I never had either one, and never will have." Her eyes bore into his soul. "Have I got anybody, Will Brite?"

His spontaneous promise to her wrenched him yet again. "I . . . I told you you deserve better than me," he said.

"Maybe I think different. Maybe I know you better than you do yourself, even this quick."

Flooded by memories he wished to erase, Will lowered his eyes, but Jessie's voice followed him into the past. "Look at me," she said. "Look at me and tell me you don't care for me."

Will did look. "Maybe I do. But that's not enough. The things I've done—"

"I don't care. I don't care about any of that. Whatever it is you're letting stand between us, just get rid of it!"

"That's just it," said Will. "How you ever get forgive for somethin'?"

"Asking might be a start."

Will seemed to smell again the burning stench in the Texarkana night. "What if there's nobody to ask no more?"

"Then ask the one that really matters."

He started to press her on who that could be, and then it dawned on him. "I don't expect He wants nothin' to do with the likes of me."

"He can forget what you done wrong. I learned as much from my mama, even though she died having me."

"How—"

"Papa tried burning everything she had once, but I raked out a Bible and kept it hid. The leather was scorched, but the pages were all there. She'd marked places just like she was talking to me. One tells about Him blotting out the bad and not remembering it."

Will had longed for forgiveness all through his journey toward punishment, but something like that had to come at a greater price than he could ever pay.

Emotion hung in his throat. "It can't be as easy as just lookin' at the sky and sayin' you're sorry."

"You've got to do your part. He'll forget, but you've got to do your part."

"My part," repeated Will. He looked down and kicked the ground. "I tell you, I know what I done, and if I'm any kind of man, I . . . I got to take what's comin' to me."

"Get your head up, Will Brite. Get your head up and look at me!"

Will knew he had no choice but to comply;

facing her was all part of his punishment.

She continued. "You act like you're doing everybody a favor. You make a mud hole out of your own guilt and you're just rolling in it. To hear you talk, everything's about you and you trying to ease your conscience about something. Well, it's not about you. There's me now and there's us. Or at least there could be an us."

Will wanted to turn away, but he couldn't, even as he began to see her through a mist.

"You . . ." His voice didn't seem to work right. "You don't have no idea how much I wish things was different."

"Have you heard anything I said? Just own up to Him for whatever it is you did wrong!"

"I *am* sorry, Jessie. And He already knows what I done."

"Maybe you are, and maybe He does. But you've still got to own up to Him. And then you've got to forgive yourself."

It didn't seem right, asking for a pardon from somebody other than those Will had wronged. If he could just start by standing face-to-face with any of them . . . confessing what he had done . . . begging forgiveness . . .

"You got no idea what I'm dealin' with," he said. "No idea what ever' day's like for me."

The moment he said it, he couldn't believe that he had just validated everything she had said about his self-centeredness. All he could do was stand before her convicted, as her face told him that she realized it too.

"How . . . How is it you know more about things than I do?" he asked contritely. "The way you been raised . . ."

He drew her to him, resting his cheek against her buoyant hair and asking himself if he was going to let her get away, this young woman he admired so much, cared for so much. He felt her arms slide around his shoulders, but now it was only he who trembled.

21

Zeke knew this couldn't keep going on.

Any day now, Quint of the Half Moons would come riding back with those suspicious eyes. Only a fool would have hung around this long waiting for the inevitable, and Zeke wondered if on some level he wanted to be caught. Could strangulation at the end of a rope be any worse than what he endured every minute of every day?

He had pondered the matter ever since Quint had gone north with a herd, and with the drovers already overdue to return, Zeke had bought himself another day to think by volunteering for this ride. That was why the deliberate drum of his bronc's hoofs echoed this very moment between the walls of Dead Man's Pass.

The truth was, Zeke didn't want to go any-where near another dead body, not when he had so many ghosts already chasing him. But he had told Will that Jessie should have the peace of mind of knowing for sure that Caleb could never hurt her again.

The blood trail had almost disappeared, but as

soon as Zeke broke past the confining bluffs and saw the buzzards circling over right-side yuccas, he figured he had all the proof anyone needed.

There were fewer rocks and more windswept alkali here, and he jumped his horse across three or four sharply eroded washes as he weaved through the daggers. He could make out a stirring of black feathers on the ground ahead, and by the time only a few shielding yuccas stood in his way, dark shadow tracks began crossing before him.

Zeke heard the flapping of wings as the vultures labored to rise, and then he was there, stricken by the mutilated body of a man.

Drawing rein and dismounting, he secured his horse and untied a shovel from his saddle. The stench was suffocating, and he slipped his bandana over his nose as he approached. Buzzards had shredded and devoured, but the face-down position gave Zeke hope of a positive identification.

Kneeling, he rolled the body over.

It was Caleb, all right, and the soaked dirt underneath showed that he had finished bleeding out before he had accomplished even a mile from where he had taken return gunfire. It was a gruesome sight, this man left for the buzzards, and Zeke hoped that somebody on the Big Red had given Master Young the proper burial he had deserved.

Zeke set to work beside the remains, the shovel digging again and again into the alkali. Caught between the relentless sun and the ground's radiating heat, he wondered which man—the dead or the live—the soaring buzzards waited for. Finally he had a shallow three-by-six, and in another minute he was shoveling dirt down in Caleb's face.

There never seemed enough soil to refill an excavation, but Zeke scooped up enough nearby to form a mound. He spent another several minutes hauling and stacking rocks, for loafer wolves were bad about digging up fresh graves. Lastly, he fashioned a crude cross out of mesquite sticks lashed together with rawhide saddle strings.

Not until Zeke drove it into place at grave's head did he realize that he had breached accepted practice: He had buried Jessie's father along a north-south axis rather than east-west.

Had it been a friend under all that dirt and rock, Zeke would have exhumed the body and reburied it the Christian way. The Lord Almighty was coming back one of these days, like lightning flashing from east to west, and when He called people up out of their graves, those properly buried would face Him immediately. But maybe it was just as well that Caleb would be looking elsewhere; Zeke figured that when the time came the wretched bastard would be doing everything he could to hide.

Suddenly it was as if that moment was already here and it was Zeke, not Caleb, rising up to shield his face. His sweet Vennie and Master Young and Major Hyler were there too, caught up beside him, but their eyes were set upon the east and shone with a glory Zeke would never know—not when he had so many things to answer for before the approaching Almighty.

I can't lets You see me! I can't! I can't!

But the Almighty *could* see, every one of his failings, no matter how hard he tried to hide them.

The clatter of the falling shovel shook Zeke back into the here and now, and he found himself staring at the ramshackle cross he had erected. Even though he had joined the limbs himself, the knotted bark strangely took on new and deeper meaning. It seemed to stream with blood, precious blood that could cover sins even as great as Zeke's.

As a wave of emotion rolled down from the Big Red and swept over him, Zeke sank to his knees before the Master's cross.

In a grove of towering pecan trees near trickling Second Crossing on the Devils, Zeke spent the most peaceful night he could remember. Maybe he hadn't squared things with the Almighty yet, or even with himself, but at least he knew some of the stops along the way. It would take a lot of courage, more than he had right now, but pushing on through his fear would be a small price considering the stakes.

He reached the flat adjacent to Beaver Lake the next afternoon to find a mounted Will meeting the drovers as they returned from delivering the first herd to the head draws of Dove and Spring creeks. This was the moment of truth, the first test of all Zeke had vowed, and his legs went to quivering even as his boots stayed in the stirrups.

He scanned the cowhands and dusty remuda for Quint of the Half Moons, and he didn't know how to feel when he didn't see him.

"Pure-dee hell, seventy-something mile each way," a mustached drover was saying as Zeke pulled up unseen at the hindquarter of Will's Appaloosa. "Just left dead cows in piles ever' step. And ever' herd after us just added to them."

"How many head you end up with?" Will asked.

"Two-thirds, I guess. Maybe less. Bad as it was when we crossed some of that same country with the wagons couple of weeks ago, it's worse now. Got a lot hotter."

"Men make it all right? Been expectin' y'all a while."

"Had to lay up on Dove Creek and rest the horses. Us too. Sun near' baked our skulls. Just dropped one hand, though, and that was after we got to the head draws."

Zeke looked the exhausted men over again. "That be Mister Quint of the Half Moons?"

Will gave a quick look back, obviously surprised to hear his voice.

"Matter of fact, it was," said the drover. "Ain't on my payroll, but surprised me, him up and ridin' off that way. Took a Half Moon horse, so don't guess it was any of my affair."

Again Will glanced at Zeke, but it was the sunburned drover that he addressed.

"We'll let you get on over to the wagons. Looks like you hadn't seen shade in a while."

"Nary a bit of it the whole way."

Zeke held his horse at the Appaloosa's flank and swallowed dust as the drovers and remuda passed. Only after they were out of earshot did Will rein his animal around to him.

"Didn't know you was anywhere on the place. What you find out?"

"I buries him the wrong way."

"You found him? Dead? What do you mean, wrong way?"

For a moment, Zeke relived his troubling experience at the grave.

"Gotta be ready, time comes. Hidin' won't do us no good."

"You feelin' all right? You say Caleb's dead?"

Will's first question had caught Zeke off-guard; he hadn't realized he had muttered his thoughts. Quickly, he gathered himself.

"Buzzards eatin' away, they was. But I could tell it was him, other side of that pass."

Will looked away for a moment, his cheek twitching. "Jessie already thinks he's dead, so maybe I oughtn't even say anything to her. Least, I'll know now when I lay down to sleep."

Will gave a troubled half-laugh and wagged his head. "Sleep! How the hell's somebody like me ever expect to sleep? Sometimes I think it'd been better if Major had come back from the snows instead of me."

"I don't know, Mister Will. Maybe you still s'posed to make things right. Maybe we both still got a chance to be lookin' east come that day."

Will looked at him strangely, but Zeke just couldn't summon the courage to say more.

22

Lately Zeke had noticed a change coming over Will. For the first several weeks of Zeke's employment, Will had seemingly done all he could to avoid him. He had tolerated Zeke, nothing more, but now the Slash Five boss was far more open to his company, and the situation reminded Zeke of his relationship with Master Young.

If Zeke needed any more confirmation, he found it when Will paired off with him the next morning as the Slash Five crew turned north up Pecos Canyon, three-quarters of a mile down-stream of Beaver Lake. Superintendent Rayburn had instructed the hands to round up this gulch, so-named "Pecos" because the old mail road veered up it en route from the Devils to the Pecos River.

Working the defile demanded that cowhands start at the uppermost limit of the cattle's range, a point dictated by the animals' need to return to the Devils for water. But there was also the necessity that the beeves find forage, meaning that the cattle had to strike a delicate balance.

By the time Zeke and Will had made five or six gently winding miles, few beeves moved among the maggot-infested carrion. The two men were the last remaining riders, the others having veered off in pairs to work each passing hollow. Throughout, the old road had been plain, deeply scored under whitewashed ledges and cacti-studded slopes. Now as Will and Zeke drew rein where the canyon forked at a limestone-capped butte, the trace continued unmistakably up a west branch with no sign of cows. The narrow gorge to the north, however, showed hides and horns stirring among scrub mesquites and algerita bushes.

Will nodded to the beeves, and soon the two cowboys were riding north side-by-side as the hoofbeats echoed between bare, rocky slopes only sixty yards apart. Except for giving orders, Will had been quiet all morning, as if deep in thought. Now, though, as thorns tugged at Zeke's leggings, Will looked over at him.

"You was talkin' kind of funny when you come back yesterday."

A scrawny jackrabbit jumped out in front of Zeke's bronc, but abruptly the black cowhand saw only the cross at the head of Caleb's grave.

"I seen it like it gonna be. I seen this colored person ashamed to show his face."

"Your face? Who from?"

"Him, Mister Will."

"Him who?"

"Come that day, won't be no place to hide, 'less I sets things right."

Will gave a sharp breath. "It's like tryin' to herd cats, talkin' to you. What day you mean?"

"The one He do the judgin'."

All the energy drained from Will's face. "Oh, that." He turned back to the onward-threading canyon and seemed to ponder for a moment. "So now you're thinkin' it can all be forgot? Who's got in your ear, Jessie? Way you been talkin', skeletons is as bad in your closet as they are in mine."

Zeke flinched to all the painful memories, and he drew rein, leading Will to do the same.

"Yes, sir, Mister Will," he said as they faced one other, "and mine's a-rattlin' more and more ever' day. They's grabbed hold of my insides, they has, and they's dragged me right up to the Boss Man and made me listen. He tellin' me, 'Ain't too late,' He says. He take me in like a mama hen do her chicks if I just lets Him. But I feels too dirty. I needs to do some things first, even scared-y cat that I am."

Will seemed more than genuinely interested. His eyes, the lines at his brow, his twitching cheek—everything in his face suggested a man seized by Zeke's every word.

"Do what kind of things?" he asked.

255

In an instant, Zeke replayed all the events since the Big Red.

"I just been runnin', I has, stompedin' from here to Jericho. And ever' time I looks up, it still right in front of me. If I 'fess up, takes what comin', maybe I feels clean enough to go in under His wing like He a-wantin'. That rope be a-tightenin' around my neck, sure 'nough, but that won't matter come judgin' day."

"Was what you done that bad?"

"Awful bad, it is, and I hoped Mister Quint of Half Moons be here yesterday so's all be over with. But he gone, so's I tells you instead, Mister Will, and you tell me what this colored person to do."

Will's eyes were penetrating. "You kill somebody, Zeke? That what you did, kill somebody?"

"I was outside a poison joint, waitin' for Master Young to come out, Big Red way. He my master once, but after the war I rides for him. His the Star Circles stuff, Rockin' J's, bunch more. Yes, sir, Mister Will, Half Moons too. He like a pappy to me, best man I ever knowed. Ever' time we take a herd somewheres, he get the gold and says, 'Zeke, you carry the money belt under you' shirt. Somebody rob us, won't never expect it on a colored person.'

"I was settin' there on that porch when a white man come out of the joint and says, 'Who's you belong to, nigger?'

" 'I rides for Master Young,' I says polite-like. I sure smells the liquor on him.

'You look like a smart nigger,' he says. 'I don't like smart niggers. I goin' to smack you one.'

" 'I don't wants no trouble,' I tells him.

"That man, he tryin' to get me to do somethin' so's he can shoot me, sure 'nough. He puts a hand on his gun and steps towards me, right straight-like. He still talkin', sayin', 'Take a swing at me, you black SOB.' I knows better, so's he yanks out his gun and goes to pistol-whippin' me.

"I just covers up and takes it. I know what happens to a colored person that hits a white man.

"Blood runnin' in my eyes, but I sees Master Young come out of that joint. He's yellin' at that man and they goes to fightin'. Gun, it go slidin' yonder across porch, and when Master Young gets knocked back and takes hold of a post, man grabs up that six-shooter and cocks it so's he can shoot him.

"I barely can sees, but I was all over him like a panther. Got my hand around that six-gun and my finger against the trigger, but he got his hands all over it too.

"Boom! Goes off like hell a-poppin', and I looks over and sees Master Young slidin' down that post. White man, he run off, and there I was, holdin' that gun and Master Young center-shot, his blood spillin' out all over them boards and people runnin' out sayin', 'Nigger killed him! Nigger killed him!'

"I jumps on my horse and rides, and I still a-goin'."

Throughout, Zeke had forced himself to look at Will; he figured it was good practice for standing before the Almighty. Now, as Zeke paused to steady himself before telling of misdeed piled upon misdeed, Will's eyes were wide, staring.

"So it *is* that," said Will. "You *are* the one. Quint told me he had his suspicions. You tellin' me the truth?"

"You knowed?" asked a stunned Zeke.

"Not lyin' to me, are you, Zeke?"

"No, sir, I swears it before Boss Man up high."

"If it happened like you say, then you didn't do nothin' wrong. You—"

"But I did, Mister Will. It was my finger pull that trigger. I killed the best man I ever knowed, just like I'd turned that forty-five on him a-purpose."

"If you're on the up-and-up with me about it," said Will, "it was a accident. You was tryin' to save him."

Zeke no longer could keep his gaze up. It fell to the saddle horn, where rested the two hands that had sent the one constant in his life to the grave.

"I don't sees it that way," he whispered through

emotion. "And none of them white folk that come runnin' out did neither."

Again, Zeke made himself bare his face and soul before the Slash Five boss.

"They's more, Mister Will. I got off with that gold. It belong to Master Young's wife, and I didn't even 'member I got it for miles and miles. It like a curse, a-hangin' over me all the way down to the Slash Fives."

"You still have it? Where—"

"I stuffs it in a dead cow. I shows you when we get back."

Will took off his hat and wiped his beaded brow against his forearm. A deep breath followed before he shook his head.

"Nobody seen the shootin' but you?" he asked.

"Just Master Young—he lookin' down from glory land now—and that white man that went a-runnin'."

"Maybe," said Will, "if they was to find him somehow—"

"Master Young and him white, I ain't. Somebody go and die, don't matter who done it. I be the one swingin'."

"You was in some kind of town, wasn't you? Maybe somebody saw . . ."

Zeke had to look down a moment to summon more courage.

"They's more, and they wasn't nobody seen it

'cept Lord A'mighty. I was a-skinnin' cows, and up rides that Half Moon man, other one that was with Mister Quint at the line shack. Hog-ties me. 'I gonna kill you, you don't give me that money,' he says. But that gold belong to Master Young's wife, and I want to get it back to her. I takes him to it and he fixin' to kill me anyhows, shut this colored person up. But I gets the drop and shoots him, hides him under all them cows."

Will went ashen. "My Lord!"

"So's now you know. They's be hangin' me twice if they could. But don't matter, long as I feels clean enough to let Him take me under His wing."

Indeed, Zeke already felt better just by telling Will; the two killings had been a frightful load for a man to carry alone.

Will, though, seemed strangely shaken.

"That what it's goin' to take?" he asked hoarsely. "Gettin' hung for us to be forgive?"

"You do somethin' worth gettin' hung for, Mister Will?"

Will wouldn't answer, and the way his head dropped as he turned away told Zeke not to press the matter. But the Slash Five boss, while still avoiding his gaze, finally volunteered quiet words that only thinly veiled a lot of emotion.

"Forgettin', forgivin', that's what Jessie says. Own up and just ask Him, she says." Will wagged his head and his words turned bitter. "Hell, what right I got to expect somebody to forgive me, much less forget what I done? How you ever feel clean when you let all those people . . ."

Will hesitated, trying to control the waver in his voice.

"I know what I done, and burnin' in hell's too good for me."

Will gigged his horse and the animal bolted, but Zeke knew the folly of trying to outrun bad memories.

Keeping his horse in an easy walk, Zeke didn't catch up with Will until they had traced a two-mile dogleg through the canyon. Coming abreast as the Slash Five boss veered into an offshoot bearing north, Zeke didn't say anything at first, but as the shrinking bluffs funneled them onward, Zeke turned to him.

"You didn't tell me what I needs to do."

Will didn't look up as his horse picked its way through tasajillo and prickly pear.

"Askin' advice from somebody that's made as many mistakes as me's not very smart," he said. "I spend most of my time second-guessin' the things I decided for myself."

Will motioned ahead. "Take this canyon here —way it's headed, I expect it's not over eighty mile, straight shot, to the Slash Fives. Bet you in

261

a day's time we'd be in some of that same country we near' froze in. That horse of Major's probably come right through here. I could've gone after him, kept goin' after him, I don't care how much he was fightin' us. Instead, I decided to turn tail and save my own hide."

"We let that good man down, all right," agreed Zeke. "He a-needin' us, even if he don't know it, and we sure let him down."

Will glanced at Zeke. "So there you have it— just how sorry anything Will Brite ever decided really is."

For another mile they rode on, raising a powdery plume that swept over nothing but dead cattle and dried cow chips. Gradually the canyon became a ribbon of a valley, with hundred-foot knolls swelling gently on either side. But no matter what one called this place, it burned as hot as any branding fire Zeke had ever felt, thanks to heat radiating from hewn boulders scattering the bottom.

It was clear that cattle no longer ranged this far, and Zeke was ready to turn back and start the roundup drive until Will pointed to a small mott of wilted live oaks ahead.

"Only shade we'll see all day," Will said. "No use wastin' it."

As they approached through a scorching wind, they rode upon a bit of linsey-woolsey cloth flying like a flag in a stirrup-high mesquite. The moment Will retrieved it from a thorn and held it up, Zeke flinched in anticipation.

"Lord A'mighty, Mister Will. Lord A'mighty, just what we was talkin' about."

Will looked at him strangely, and then the implications seemed to dawn on him. He was the first to urge his horse forward, but Zeke did so too, leaning over one way and then the other as he scoured the ground at the working hoofs.

A few yards ahead they found a muslin sack clinging by its drawstring to a tasajillo, and then cigarette papers fluttering from the spines of prickly pear. As they went farther, a regular trail of items marked the dust—an unspent match, a shredded neckerchief, a leather war bag, a glinting tobacco tin. But it was the familiar hat, caught up in daggered lechuguilla, that told Zeke his suspicions were right.

Under a stunted live oak twisting up against a chiseled boulder that would have protected against snow drifts, they found him. There wasn't much left, after the scavengers of winter and the ants and sun of spring, but the initials stenciled on the belt left no doubt.

"My Lord," said a stunned Will. "My Lord, Major, it's you."

Zeke dismounted, but Will was too troubled to do more than shake his bowed head. Zeke took a step toward the scattered remains, but couldn't bring himself to go any closer. Reverently, he removed his hat and stared, seeing Master Young as much as he did the long-missing manager of the Slash Fives.

"I . . . I buries him right, so's he be ready."

Will's voice began to quake from the saddle.

"Him off to war and his wife dies, and it's all his fault, least to him. Pillar to post all those years, just lookin' for—what would Arch call it? Redemption?"

Will breathed sharply, bitterly. "Well, there wasn't no redemption—not for him or me neither. He had to run off and die like her, 'cause there wasn't nothin' else he could do. I find a big enough fire, be nothin' else for me either."

23

Have I got anybody, Will Brite? Have I got anybody?

All during the roundup drive back to Beaver Lake, Jessie's words seemed to echo from every canyon wall. Why wouldn't Will accept her into his arms? If he was just biding his time for a chance to die like all those Negroes, why couldn't it be from inside her embrace?

Jessie.

Will had nothing else. He wanted nothing else, except the things he could never have.

He remembered the first real talk they'd had, down behind a giant live oak at the lake, and relived the giddiness. He yearned for that feeling again and realized it was still there, buried under all the guilt.

Will hated himself, all right, but did he hate himself enough to give all that up?

It was midday by the time he and the cowhands reached Beaver Lake and threw the Pecos Canyon beeves in with the roundup herd. As Will rode into camp, he found the cook rummaging in the chuck box as something bubbled in a cast iron pot at the fire. On a pallet at the back wagon wheel, someone he almost didn't recognize sat bent over a plate of beans.

"Arch?" Will asked in astonishment as he neared. "That you?"

Arch looked up, showing normal color in a face all too gaunt.

"What remains of him. The manner in which my heart is achin' for bacon, one would think I had deprived myself of the king's delicacies for nigh onto a fortnight."

Will's spirits rose in a way he hadn't thought possible.

"Good old Arch!" He placed a hand on the man's shoulder as though welcoming him home. "Still spoutin' lingo I can't understand. How you doin'?"

"I seemed to have misplaced a week or ten, all except for fleeting glimpses of an angel."

"A angel?"

"A regular cherub, or was it seraphim? But when I woke up this morning, it was neither. No angel of mercy ever presented that degree of grace and beauty."

"You must mean Jessie."

"Ah, yes, Jessie, the most beauteous creature who ever walked God's Earth."

"This is the devil's country, case you forgot."

Arch's eyes sparkled. "Then the contrast makes

her all the more wondrous. I think Cupid's arrow has struck this cowboy right in the heart."

"Watch it, Arch. Not all of us been sleepin' all this time."

"You mean—?"

"I mean she's took."

Just like that, Will decided, and as his giddiness soared to strange new heights, he suddenly couldn't wait to see her.

"Where is she?" he asked excitedly with a quick scan of camp.

"Over at the cabin. Will, I do believe that you've broken this poet's heart."

"Some poet you are. A poet would've drowned himself in words instead of water."

Arch feigned a sniffle and brushed an imaginary tear from his eye. "Words, water, tears. I've drowned in them all now."

Will started to turn away for the cabin, and then realized that Arch needed to know about Pecos Canyon.

"Arch, got somethin' to tell you when you're feelin' stronger."

The cowhand started to ask, but Will tried to fend him off with a raised palm. Still, Arch persisted.

"I perceive it in your expression, Will," he said solemnly. "You found Major, didn't you."

"I'll tell you about it later," Will said. "Got a angel of my own to see after."

• • •

Five minutes later, Will mounted the line-shack step.

"You in here, Jessie?"

There was no answer, but as soon as Will went through the open door and looked toward Caleb's bed, he saw her standing there, looking much the same as when he had first seen her—barefoot in a simple cotton dress, her dangling curls accentuating mysterious, dark eyes. Their gazes met, and her shoulders immediately sagged in a troubling gesture.

"What are you doin' here?" he asked.

Her reply had a tone of surrender.

"Where you expect me to be? The man that beat me's dead, your friend's up and about, and you . . ."

For a couple of seconds she stared, and then she looked down, searching for words or strength but finding only a whisper.

"All my life . . ."

Her voice failed, and Will didn't know what to do except speak her name and reach for her. He was shocked when she recoiled at his touch, her eyes flashing up angrily.

"A dead end, that's what it's been," she snapped. "I'm through with dead ends. That's a road I'm not going down anymore. You want to wallow in self-pity? Well, go ahead, Will Brite, but I'm not doing it with you. *Have* your pity and

268

your guilt! Because that's all you're ever going to have."

She whirled to Caleb's bed and began stripping it, a dust devil of rage, clawing and throwing.

"It's you I want, Jessie."

Will placed his hands on her shoulders from behind, but she jerked away and redoubled her efforts. A blanket caught on a broken spring, but she pulled violently as it ripped.

"Jessie, listen to me."

Still, the blanket held fast, even as she continued to rend. Once more Will reached for her, and this time as she pulled away, she fell across the bed and buried her face in the tatters. Her shoulders began to shake, and Will abruptly saw everything through a mist.

He went closer, never in his life wanting anything more than just to hold her. If she would just hear him out . . . give him another chance . . . give both of them another chance . . .

"Jessie . . ."

Now his own voice didn't want to work, but he forced it to.

"Jessie, ever'thing you said about me's right. It's me I been thinkin' of, not nobody else. I got all these memories and I just been lettin' them take over and keep me from livin'. I been afraid to live, 'cause I didn't think I had any reason to. Well, you've give me a reason."

Through a blur he saw her come to an elbow

and turn to him, and he wasn't ashamed to let her see his burning eyes and quaking jaw.

"That's what I come over to tell you," he continued. "What went on all those years ago's not ever goin' to change. It's with me and I guess it always will be. But I give you my word, right here and now, I'm through lettin' it take over. Maybe that's not enough. Maybe I'm too late. But I'll always love you, Jessie, even if I never see you no more."

Jessie stared at him for so long that Will wondered if there was anything about him she couldn't see.

"Don't you dare, Will Brite," she finally said. "Don't you dare say you love me unless you do. Don't you dare!"

Will went closer and stretched out a tentative arm. "I'd never lie to you, Jessie."

Her eyes continued to probe, and then her hand stole out for his.

"You better not hurt me, Will Brite."

For a split second before his hand closed on hers, he thought about a fire big enough to die in.

24

Zeke didn't know what else to do right now, so he kept going about his work with a cowboy's sense of duty.

In this one-of-a-kind cow hunt, a cowboy had plenty to keep him busy, even if he was just part of a three-hundred-man army. In the hands of a boss less capable than Rayburn, that many riders could have tripped over one another, but everything proceeded like the second hand of Master Young's gold watch.

The Slash Five's assignment was to work the canyons as far down as Pecan Springs and push the beeves back up to Beaver Lake. From there, other cowboys would head out each morning with another two thousand freshly watered animals, fated either to mark the trail with their bleaching bones, or to reach Dove or Spring Creeks after eighty hours of day-and-night travel and await the general roundup there.

Day after day, Zeke scoured the Devils' recesses for cattle still capable of making the march. He rounded up without regard for brand, of course, and Lord knows, he always found more dead beeves than live ones. But he always took special satisfaction in turning a Slash Five animal back toward Beaver Lake in the first leg of its journey home. Major Hyler had died trying to save the Slash Five herd, and Zeke could think of no better way to honor his memory.

At times, Zeke found himself envying the very cattle whose lives so depended on him. Cattle spent their days concerned only with forage and water, not with regret or guilt or judgment. In their ignorant bliss, they were probably a whole lot happier, even if they didn't know what happiness was.

When the trap door finally would spring, maybe Zeke would experience it too, if only for a split second.

On yet another searing morning, Zeke pondered such things as he worked Johnsons Run, a west-lying gulch that intersected Devils Canyon six miles below Beaver Lake. The sky with its tracing vultures had an unusual look today, not the typical reddish brown of suspended dust but a deathly gray pallor that denied Zeke a dark shadow. He had flushed a half-dozen Slash Five steers out of the scrub mesquites already, and as he drove them toward the Devils he hoped Major Hyler looked down in approval from somewhere above that haze.

Just as Zeke rubbed his dripping brow into his

shoulder, curving horns broke through catclaw and algerita bushes that filled a narrow, right-side gorge. Behind came speckled hide, and then more horns, framed by the canyon's soaring rock columns with clinging cacti. Trailing the beeves was a bleeding bay with Will in the saddle.

"Thorns get you?" asked Zeke as they threw the two bunches together.

Will glanced at the sky as he fell in beside Zeke. "Funny weather we're havin'. Yeah, that catclaw makes you glad you got your leggin's, all right."

Zeke looked at his own chaps draped over his boot tops. "You' feet ever bothers you like mine?"

"All time, around the toes. I'm thinkin' Arch might be right about losin' some come June."

Zeke shuddered as reality gripped him. "We get these cows home, expect I be losin' a whole lot more than wigglers."

Hoofs plodded onward for several seconds before Zeke realized that Will stared at him.

"I be goin' to the law," explained Zeke as they faced one another. "Start makin' things right."

"Zeke, they'll hang you."

"Yes, sir, Mister Will, they's make this colored person dance, all right. But I want to feel a smile on my face, like I been seein' on you."

Will suddenly seemed both troubled and embarrassed, and he turned back to the speckled rumps ahead.

"Didn't know it showed."

"A good thing to see, Mister Will. Miss Jessie, she a-smilin' too."

"Guess you put two and two together," said Will.

"Feet a-hurtin', but eyes healed up good."

Will rode in silence for a full minute, his profile framed against the far canyon slope.

"When work's done here, I'm takin' her back with me," he said.

Vennie! Vennie! Sweet Vennie!

The name suddenly bounced through every nook of Zeke's mind and seemed to echo between the cacti-strewn bluffs of Johnsons Run. What had worked out for Will would never work out for Zeke. He would never see Vennie again. He would never look into her eyes or hear her tender whispers or know the happiness of being in her arms. Not ever!

"I . . . sure glad for you, Mister Will. Miss Jessie, she a fine woman."

"Goin' to marry her, Zeke. Don't know why she'd have me, but I'm goin' to marry her."

"You doin' a good thing by Miss Jessie. Lots of white folk wouldn't ever think of marryin' thataway."

"What do you mean?"

It had slipped out so casually that Zeke was stunned to realize that he had said it. Now, as he found all kinds of confusion in Will's face, he didn't know what to say.

"Zeke," Will pressed, "what are you talkin' about?"

Abruptly Will reined up, and Zeke felt obliged to do so as well.

"I talks too much, Mister Will. You and Miss Jessie gonna be happy."

Zeke turned to urge his horse on again, but Will wouldn't let the matter go.

"Hold on. That's the second time you said somethin' funny like that. You was talkin' about the two of you's grandfathers gettin' beat."

Zeke didn't like where this was headed. He nodded to the beeves. "They's gonna turn back, we ain't careful."

This time Zeke squeezed the horse with his thighs, but a hand darted out and seized the bridle. Whirling, Zeke found Will's face determined, his eyes piercing.

"You're not goin' anywhere till you talk to me."

"Let me ride on, Mister Will," Zeke pleaded. "I don't want to put nothin' between you and Miss Jessie."

Will's face had never looked so flushed. "You're stayin' right here. Damn it, tell me straight out."

"Ask Miss Jessie," Zeke begged.

"Straight out, I said!"

"She a mulatto, like my own mama."

"A what? Isn't that Mex talk? Young mule or somethin'?"

Zeke wished he were already climbing the gallows.

"She colored, Mister Will."

Will went as ashen as the limestone bluffs behind him. "You crazy? What the hell's the matter with you?"

"She pass for white, but Miss Jessie colored like I is."

Will's cheek twitched, the veins at his temple looking ready to burst.

"You son of a bitch, you lie about her that way and I'll knock you off your damned horse!"

"Do it matter, Mister Will? If you love her, do it matter?"

Wheeling his bay, Will bumped Zeke's animal hard in the shoulder, spooking it. Rocked, Zeke turned to pull the bronc's head up and saw Will's flashing fist out of the corner of his eye. The next thing Zeke knew, he was down in prickly pear, and little specks of light were flying everywhere.

"Hyaah!"

Dazed, Zeke looked up to see Will scattering the beeves as he spurred his horse toward Devils River.

The screams of all those Negroes—a mother, a father, so many little children—roared in Will's ears like the hellish flames he had helped kindle.

The forelegs of the bay reached out again and

again, the hoofbeats reverberating through Johnsons Run, but he couldn't outrace the memories. They were stronger than ever, frightful reminders of his lost soul as they rose up in judgment from a mass grave. For two decades they had been vague figures writhing in a fire, but now the blaze raged vividly with the features of not only Zeke, but Jessie, a dark angel sent to exact vengeance even as she teased happiness.

No! No! God, no!

It was more than Will could bear, even as he realized that no punishment could ever be enough. All he wanted was to die, to go on to hell, to have every last memory burned from his tortured mind.

At the mouth of Johnsons Run, his horse stumbled and almost went down in the white gravel of the dry Devils. But he kept the animal at a breakneck pace on to the far bank and turned up-canyon, not caring which of them died first.

As Will bore almost due north into a stout wind, he could see a great, grayish-white plume rising over distant ridges ahead. It changed shape even as he watched, one edge drifting, spreading, blanketing the horizon. Within another mile he caught a pungent whiff, and he suddenly understood the peculiar haze that left the sun hanging dim in the sky. Somewhere on the divide between the Devils and the Concho—the very area in which winter clouds had built for day after day even as drouth blighted the land elsewhere—a great range fire burned.

He wondered if somebody had built it just for him.

In minutes Will was back at the line shack and stepping off his horse with a full twist that threw him in a run for the door. He burst in, breathless and desperate, whirling one way and then another.

"What's wrong?" cried Jessie.

She stood behind the wood-burning heater, the stove pipe partially hiding her flour-smudged face as she held a cast iron skillet. She stepped aside and he stared at her, trying to reconcile her curls, her complexion, the shape of her nose and lips.

"Is it like he says? God, Jessie, is it like he says?"

Her face showed confusion, concern—or did she continue to tease?

"Tell me, Jessie. God, just tell me!"

"Will Brite—"

With a shudder, he abruptly recognized the distinguishing racial characteristics, so obvious in her features yet so muted. Now, greater emotion than ever crippled his voice.

"Why didn't you say somethin'?"

She started toward him. "Say what? You're worrying me!"

He threw a palm out, discouraging her.

"God, you're like all of them was. All those children screamin'—God, Jessie, you're colored like them."

"What children? Don't scare me this way!"

"I just let them burn up, the whole family just burn up, and now you come along, colored like they was."

"You're not making sense. What about burn? But you know how Papa treated me. You rather I come from somebody like him?"

He turned away, seeing the planks at his boots through a mist. He felt her hand on his shoulder and, try as he might, he couldn't force himself to push her away.

"So Mama found somebody that treated her good—so *what* if he wasn't white?" Jessie continued. "He must've loved her, same as I do you."

Now, the emotion didn't just choke Will's throat, it threatened to wring the last ounce of life from his dark soul. He began to weep, his words quaking.

"You don't understand, couldn't understand. I been runnin' so far, so long, just tryin' to get away from it. Ten years old, pourin' kerosene on that shack. 'Better this way,' my old man kept sayin'. 'Ain't slaves of mine no more. Got freed, they did. Can't fend for themselves and I can't take care of them. Be roamin' the whole country, gangin' up, takin' it over, stealin' what people don't give them. . . . Better this way,' he kept sayin'."

Will turned but found her face only a blur. "I helped kill them, Jessie, and you and Zeke been sent to keep on remindin' me, punishin' me, all the way to hell."

"If you was ten, it wasn't your fault, whatever you did, not any more than it's mine who my father was."

"I knowed better and I let him do it anyway. God, don't you see that? There's nobody to say I'm sorry to—nobody!"

"You promised, Will Brite. You gave me your word as a man you wouldn't let your guilt come between us anymore."

"What do I know about bein' a man? If I can't live like one, maybe I . . . I can at least—"

He spun to the door, her hands sliding across his shoulders.

"You come back here, Will Brite!" she pleaded.

But he was already outside and running for his horse, determined to find a fire big enough to die in.

25

Zeke hadn't been this troubled since he had tasted Judgment Day at Caleb's grave.

He nursed a bloody lip as he drove his beeves down Johnsons Run and joined them with other bunches at every side canyon. He ignored the other riders as they fell in beside him, for now he had accidentally wronged two more people and he had to figure out what to do.

Lost in thought, he dropped off the pace, and it was a wonder he saw Quint of the Half Moons and the puffy-cheeked stranger at all.

Zeke was abreast a lone live oak at the confluence with Devils Canyon, and the cattle were spilling down into the dry river's white-washed rubble. Fifty yards beyond, moving from right to left, the two horsemen traced the old mail road upriver toward Beaver Lake. The young stranger with the bushy mustache and the dark trousers stuffed inside knee-high boots looked loaded for bear—a bone-handled knife and a butt-forward revolver at his hip, the wood of a rifle in a saddle scabbard, a row of shining cartridges in his belt. A war bag, a bedroll, and the coil of a rope completed his equipment.

But it was what glinted on the breast of his raven wool shirt that gave Zeke pause. Maybe he presumed a little from this far away, but it looked to be what Master Young had called a cinco peso, for from that Mexican coin the State of Texas had cut a circled star. It was the badge of a Texas Ranger, and the fact that he rode with Quint told Zeke all he needed to know.

Zeke couldn't understand why they would come from the south—he supposed they had traveled by train to the Southern Pacific station below Dead Man's Pass—but they were here now, and everything was coming to a head. All he had to do was hail them and begin the long ride back to the hangman and his rope and the redemption he so needed.

But he couldn't. Not yet. Not when he had added one more thing that he had to make right.

Zeke cut his horse behind the live oak and ducked in under low-hanging limbs that scraped his hat. He was the only Negro in the entire roundup, and he would stick out like a sore thumb even at a distance. Through the blighted leaves he saw the ranger give the emerging cowhands a good look, and then continue up-canyon with Quint. Zeke's fellow drovers, meanwhile, seemed not to have noticed that Zeke had disappeared.

For long minutes, he watched Cinco Peso and

Quint repeatedly drop out of sight and reappear as they negotiated river crossings, until finally, three miles away in a haze, the moving specks vanished behind a canyon fold. Only then did Zeke take his horse on toward Beaver Lake and a faraway cloud that he recognized as smoke from a range fire on the divide. Whatever Zeke had to do to make amends for his latest wrong, it had to start with seeing Will and Jessie, but it wouldn't be easy with Cinco Peso waiting at camp.

As he rode, Zeke thought he could taste the hanging smoke, though it was difficult to distinguish in the reek of rotting carcasses. But the thunderhead of gray was plain enough, a towering column feathering down on one side to smother a wide swath of horizon.

Zeke hugged the wide canyon's east bluff as long as he could, letting its long curve hide him from Beaver Lake. But when he came opposite the broad mouth of Pecos Canyon, he drew rein, realizing almost too late that to go farther by daylight was fool's play. The last mile to the lake would be across an open flat, and all he could do for now was fade away into a recess and wait for nightfall.

Then Zeke noticed a small plume of dust approaching from the direction of camp, and he held his roan to watch curiously. Whoever it was had the horse in a gallop, and even at a distance Zeke could hear the cadence of hoofs.

The rider had come within two hundred yards and was cutting toward Pecos Canyon before Zeke realized it was Jessie. He was surprised to see her riding astride rather than by sidesaddle, but everything about her flight spoke of desperation, something Zeke knew all too much about. She was in trouble—maybe even because of him—and that was all the reason he needed to throw caution to the wind.

With a shout, Zeke gigged his roan out from behind the bluff to try to head her off. Crossing the dead river with its loose gravel slowed him, but he continued to call after her as he coaxed his mount to greater speed. Finally she looked over her shoulder and evidently recognized him, for she wheeled the sorrel and advanced to meet him.

"It's Will Brite!" she cried even before they came abreast. Her hair was wind-blown, her distraught face glistening. "I'm worried, the way he was talking! I watched him turn up Pecos Canyon! I've been all this time finding a horse!"

"All my doin', Miss Jessie. Sorry, I awful sorry."

"What do you mean?"

Just then a rifle boomed and something whizzed by overhead, the kind of thing a warning shot would do. Whirling to Beaver Lake, Zeke saw two charging figures raising dust a few hundred yards away. If the shot didn't tell Zeke enough, the flash of light from the breast of the lead rider did.

"What are they doing?" exclaimed Jessie.

"Must've seen you' dust and come out to look. Now they's seen me. Ride, Miss Jessie! We gotta catch Mister Will!"

Will didn't ride alone. All the dark faces—guiltless faces scored with the struggles common to all peoples—went with him up snaking Pecos Canyon, into one offshoot and then a second, on to the three-by-six pile of rocks that showed the folly of any hope of redemption.

At the crude cross Zeke had erected for Major, Will dismounted, realizing the jaded animal might otherwise drop dead and strand him long miles from the burn. Even now the fire could be racing toward a drouth-stricken area that would snuff out his chance for a fitting end.

Jessie! Jessie!

Her name came to him abruptly, powerfully. Of all Will's regrets, she was the greatest. His father's onetime slaves . . . Zeke . . . Major . . . They all occupied places of gloom in his remorse, but none of them haunted the way she did. From how deep in Lucifer's pit had that kind of punishment been summoned up for him? Why did she have to be everything she was—his love, his only love through a lonely journey that had taken a lifetime, and in the same instant a heartless, damning reminder?

He remembered the times in her arms, blessed

moments that heightened his despondency, and he turned his face to the sky and cried out a despairing man's cry that rolled through the shallow valley and echoed from the hills.

Mounting up, he rode on, navigating a rolling country broken by sinuous arroyos thick with mesquite and catclaw. From rocky knolls, lonesome yucca and junipers watched mutely, not caring that his load grew heavier with every strike of his horse's hoofs. The pressures were unbearable, even for a man riding to his doom, and he sagged across the saddle horn and wet the bay's mane with his face.

He pictured Jessie and Zeke, Arch and Rayburn, even Wampus and the other Slash Five riders, and pondered what they would think of him, this man brave enough to die yet too cowardly to live.

Coward!

It was the worst thing anybody could say about a cowboy, the worst legacy he could leave. If he just had a reason to turn back, to learn to live again . . . If he could just find somebody to say he was sorry to for what he had done to all those guiltless people . . .

Dusk came on before it should have, the obscuring smoke throwing an ominous yellow tinge across grassy range that was a starving cow's dream. It thrived with bluestem and dropseed, mesquite grass and sprangletop, all of such heavy growth that the stems couldn't support their own weight. They lay bunched and dry among rocks and prickly pear, a tinder box waiting to erupt.

At last light a steep slope loomed up across his path, and he took his horse on up and broke out over rim rock to face a wind dark with swirls. His eyes watered and something acrid caught in his throat, but the ash he tried to breathe was even worse.

The smoke was like inky midnight, but at ten o'clock on the flat ahead was a strange glow that reminded him of sunset fighting through a dust blizzard. Reining the bay for it, he flinched to a live ember in his eye, and when he instinctively dropped his head he saw a half-dozen tiny fires breaking out around him. His bay began to resist, but he spurred it into submission and pushed on, dodging one flare-up after another.

The wind didn't seem to know which direction to go, but it blew with a fury, sweeping the young flames this way and that. Suddenly there was nothing ahead but charred ground and pulsating coals, the blight in the wake of a consuming burn. The smoke was choking now, even as it showed the intensifying glow better, and the horse cold-jawed, wanting nothing more to do with this. When spurring didn't work, Will took the stiff handle of his quirt to its head in a way a cowboy with a soul never should.

He managed only to reach another stretch of

untouched grass before a wall of fire rose up before him, stark and blinding against the falling night. It dwarfed him even astride the bay, the yellow flames dancing and leaping before the pony's ears in an unholy ritual that must have been like perdition itself. They twisted one way and then another, roaring and throwing a boiling cloud of black into a hidden sky.

Will couldn't breathe, couldn't hear his own gagging coughs, but he could feel the searing heat that must have peeled his hide.

And he could see. He saw faces, wispy and ghostly in the blaze, the faces of the innocent straight out of that Texarkana night. They were in there, waiting and beckoning, just as they had for twenty terrible years.

With an answering cry, Will threw up a shielding arm and charged his horse for hell.

26

Zeke was caught between a wrong he still needed to right and an escort to premature judgment.

Even as Jessie's horse faltered and their lead over Cinco Peso and Quint dwindled, he tracked Will up past Major's grave and on into the watershed's smoke-filled reaches. As the desperate race slowed to a test of endurance, he explained to Jessie that a ranger was in chase, prompting a half-dozen questions from her.

"Please don't be askin', Miss Jessie," he pleaded.

Jessie in turn related a vivid and awful story of a ten-year-old boy and his father, a colored family and a fire—and Zeke no longer had need for questions. Finally he understood everything, all the way back to the first strange look Will had given him at that tangle of barbed wire.

They rode into dusk, finding their pursuers closer every time the terrain allowed a glimpse. Even when Will's trail faded in the shadows, Zeke pressed on, guided by instinct. Negotiating a steep incline a little ahead of Jessie, Zeke broke over an ash-covered rim into suffocating smoke. Spot fires were everywhere, the flames tossing in a gusting wind, but it was what Zeke saw at ten o'clock that made him wonder if Will had led him straight into Judgment Day.

From about where the horizon should have been, and halfway up the heavens, the sky burned with a strange reddish hue. It seemed a living thing, pulsing and shifting with purpose, and Zeke would have turned and fled if the shrouding smoke hadn't parted for a few fleeting seconds.

Outlined against that burst of light was a rider, so small and frail by comparison but nevertheless launching an attack against it. The silhouetted horse bolted only a few strides before the animal suddenly reared and threw the figure, and then the smoke closed again as blinding as ever.

"There!"

At the same moment that Jessie cried out, Zeke slapped spurs against horsehide and the roan jumped into a run, avoiding a small fire and then another and another. The panicky animal fought against the bit, but Zeke drew upon spur and quirt and all his horse know-how to keep it barreling through the rolling clouds of soot and ash. Hoofs beat against grassy turf and then charred ground, and just as the forelegs broke through to untouched grass again, Zeke saw Will dead ahead through smoky wisps.

Will sprawled on his stomach before a

mountain of fire, a puny man against a force not to be denied. At the whim of swirling winds, the blaze whipped wildly, yellow and orange tongues eating away at the night. Like a predator on the prowl, it suddenly seemed to sight Will, who lay shaking his head pitifully as if trying to restore his senses.

With a louder roar than ever, the fire turned and charged.

"Mister Will!"

Zeke couldn't hear his own cry, but he could feel the raging heat as he fought to keep the roan on course. A man or horse could get only so close to such a blaze, and he figured they were both past their limits when the frantic hoofs came up alongside Will. The firestorm had already coiled to pounce as Zeke reached down and seized him by the belt, but in another instant Zeke had the horse in a run and was dragging him away. Even so, Zeke wasn't sure who would win this race, but when the wind shifted again and he cut across burned ground, he realized they would make it.

Coughing and gasping, Zeke fell off the horse as soon as he pulled rein in an area relatively free of smoke. Will wheezed as well, and the two of them were side-by-side on hands and knees when Jessie rode up crying Will's name. Another moment and she was down at Will's side, embracing and sobbing, his name still on her lips.

Will seemed to find his senses and his breath at the same time, and he tried futilely to shed her arms.

"I'm not letting loose!" she cried. "You hear me? I'm not ever letting loose!"

"Jessie . . . Jessie . . ."

He started to reach for her cheek, and then drew back.

"You don't understand, Jessie—I . . . I've got to go. They're waitin' for me . . . They're in there waitin' for me . . . I've got to go!"

"Listen to me, Will Brite. Have you got your wits about you? Listen to me! Maybe He didn't send Zeke and me to punish you. Maybe He sent us so you'd have somebody to say you're sorry to."

He seemed struck by what she had said, and his jaw began to quiver as he studied her in the orange twilight. Then he looked at Zeke and back at her again, and he began to weep uncontrollably.

"I *am* sorry," he told them. "I *am, I am.* God forgive me! What I did to y'all's people—you don't have no idea how sorry I really am!"

"Then get on your feet and walk with me, Will Brite. You've took the first step already. We'll walk through this together, and you'll learn how to forgive yourself, because everybody else already has."

Will did struggle up, with her help, and as Zeke

rose too, he saw them standing arm-in-arm against the glow of the fire—a great and good union rescued out of hell.

"Move and I'll shoot!"

The strange voice exploded out of nowhere, and Zeke whirled to find two riders emerging from the young night.

"Your hands!"

With all that had happened, Zeke had almost forgotten, but he gladly extended both arms, his wrists close-set for shackles he couldn't even see yet.

"I ready for you now."

Will stepped forward, a little unsteady on his feet. "What the hell?"

"They's Mister Quint and Cinco Peso come for me," said Zeke.

"Texas Ranger," corrected the man with the shining badge as he dismounted with a leveled revolver. "Hell of a ride you been on, Zeke Boles."

Jessie rushed up beside Will. "What did he do?"

"Let him go," Will told the ranger as Zeke felt the bite of handcuffs. "He didn't do nothin' wrong."

"Always say that, don't they?"

"This time it's true. You're throwin' cuffs on somebody good enough to ride the river with. He's done more for me than any man there is."

"Yeah, well, that's what they make courts for, isn't it?"

Will looked up at the figure who still sat timidly on his horse.

"This your doin', Quint? Maybe I'll ride back with you, make *sure* he makes it to court." And then to Zeke, "Me and Jessie will do ever'thing we can for you."

Cinco Peso already had him by the arm, but that didn't keep Zeke from finding the firelight in Will's eyes.

"Don't you worry—you neither, Miss Jessie," he said with a smile. "I be all right now. I be able to show my face come that day. Both of us, Mister Will."

All of Will's emotion returned, and he placed a caring hand on Zeke's shoulder as only Master Young had ever done.

"It's not 'Mister,' Zeke. It's just 'Will.' "

About the Author

Patrick Dearen is the author of twenty-one books, including twelve novels. A native of Sterling City, Texas, he earned a bachelor of journalism from the University of Texas in 1974 and received several awards as a reporter for two West Texas daily newspapers.

A recognized authority on the Devils and Pecos Rivers of Texas, Dearen is the author of *Devils River: Treacherous Twin to the Pecos*, a history of the Devils from 1535 to 1900. He has also preserved the stories of the last generation of cowhands who plied their trade before mechanization. His research has led to nonfiction books such as *Crossing Rio Pecos*, *The Last of the Old-Time Cowboys*, and *Saddling Up Anyway*.

Dearen's novels include *To Hell or the Pecos*, winner of the West Texas Historical Association's Elmer Kelton Award and a finalist for the Will Rogers Medallion Award. His other novels include *When Cowboys Die* (a finalist for the Spur Award of Western Writers of America), *The Illegal Man* (the story of an illegal Mexican alien), and *Perseverance* (an account of hobo life in Depression-era Texas). He is a three-time winner of book awards from the West Texas

Historical Association and has also been honored by the San Antonio Conservation Society and Permian Historical Society.

A ragtime pianist and backpacking enthusiast, Dearen makes his home in Midland, Texas, with his wife Mary and their son Wesley.

Center Point Large Print
600 Brooks Road / PO Box 1
Thorndike, ME 04986-0001 USA

(207) 568-3717

US & Canada:
1 800 929-9108
www.centerpointlargeprint.com